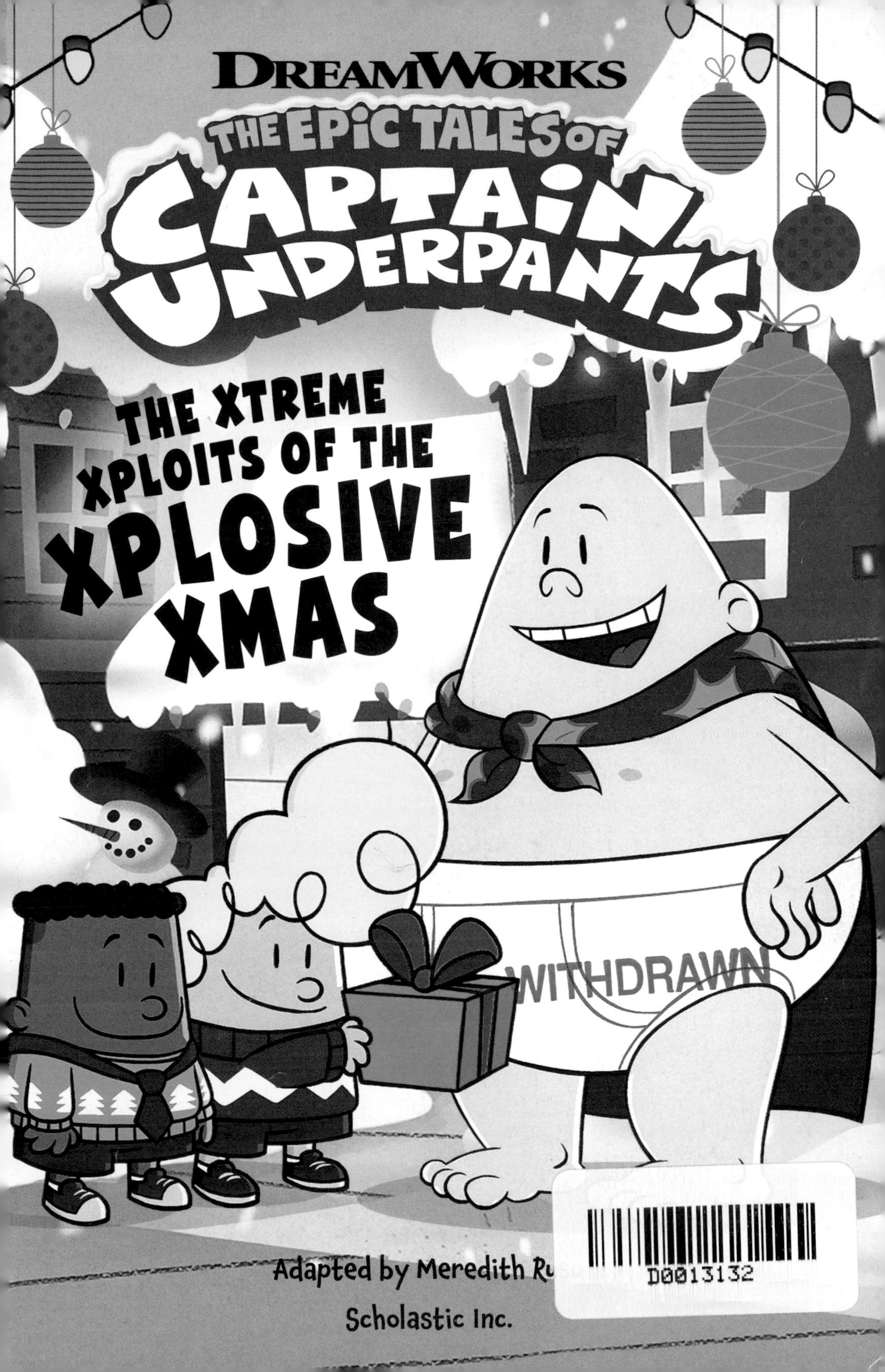
DREAMWORKS
THE EPIC TALES OF
CAPTAIN UNDERPANTS
THE XTREME XPLOITS OF THE XPLOSIVE XMAS
Adapted by Meredith Ru
Scholastic Inc.

ISBN 978-1-338-75379-0

10 9 8 7 6 5 4 3 2 1 21 22 23 24 25

Printed in the U.S.A. 40

First printing 2021

Book design by Erin McMahon

This is *George* Beard and Harold Hutchins.
GEORGE is the kid on the left with the tie and the Santa hat. **HAROLD** is the one on the right with the reindeer antlers and the bad haircut. Remember that now. George and Harold are getting their Christmas on like a holiday movie marathon because they love this time of year!

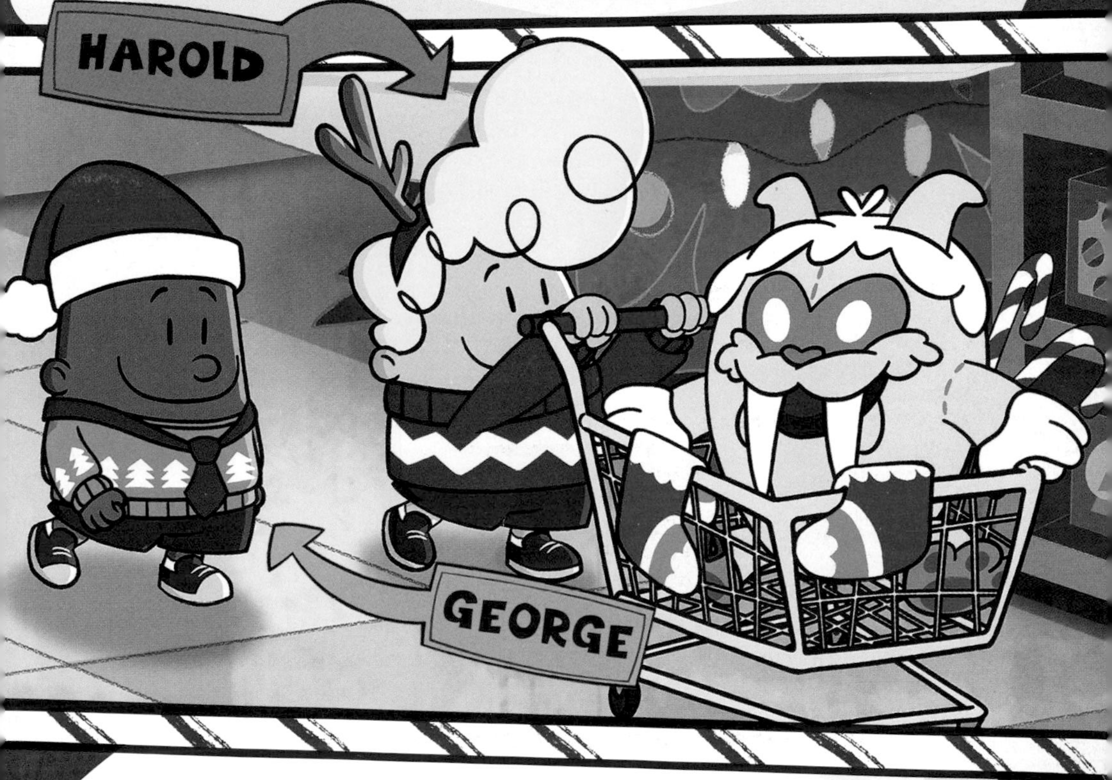
HAROLD
GEORGE

But while visions of sugarplums dance in most kids' heads, George and Harold have an epic idea to reinvent Christmas as the most pumped-up holiday ever. And thus begins our heartwarming holiday story,

THE XTREME XPLOITS OF THE XPLOSIVE XMAS.

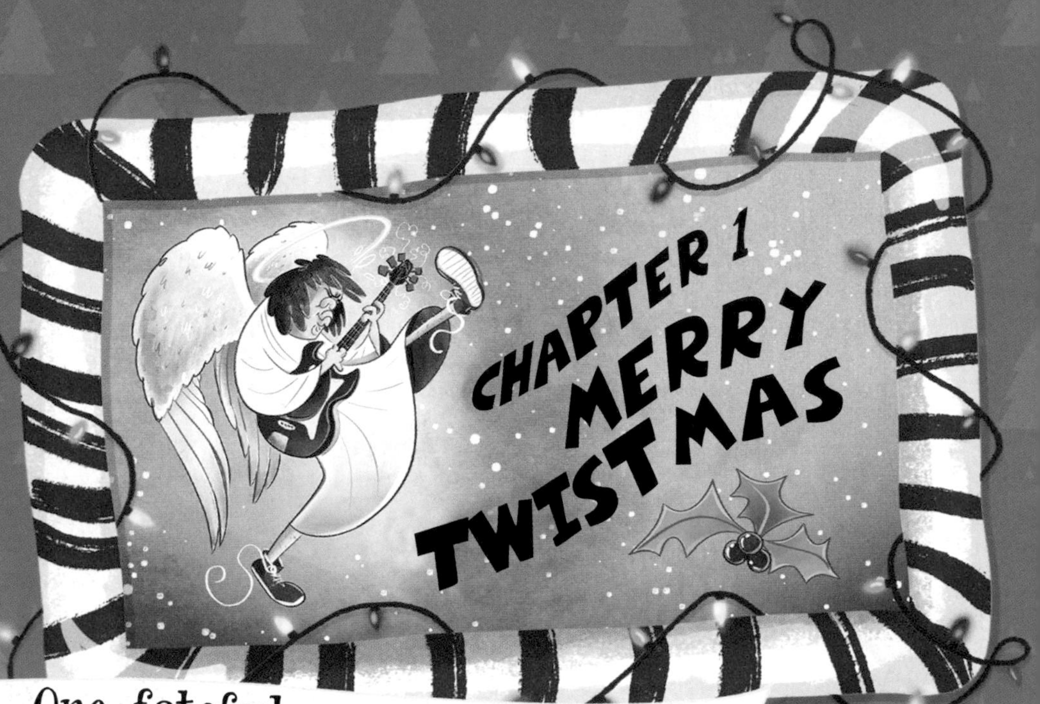
CHAPTER 1
MERRY TWISTMAS

One fateful snowy morning two weeks before Christmas . . .

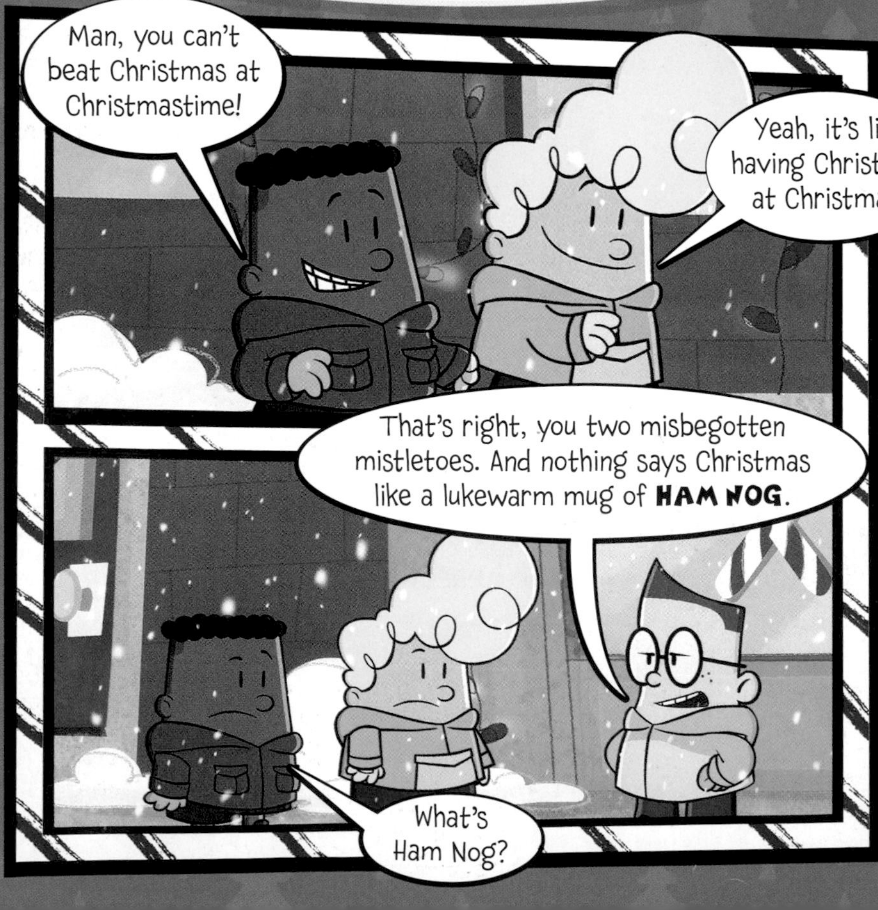
Man, you can't beat Christmas at Christmastime!
Yeah, it's like having Christmas at Christmas!
That's right, you two misbegotten mistletoes. And nothing says Christmas like a lukewarm mug of HAM NOG.
What's Ham Nog?

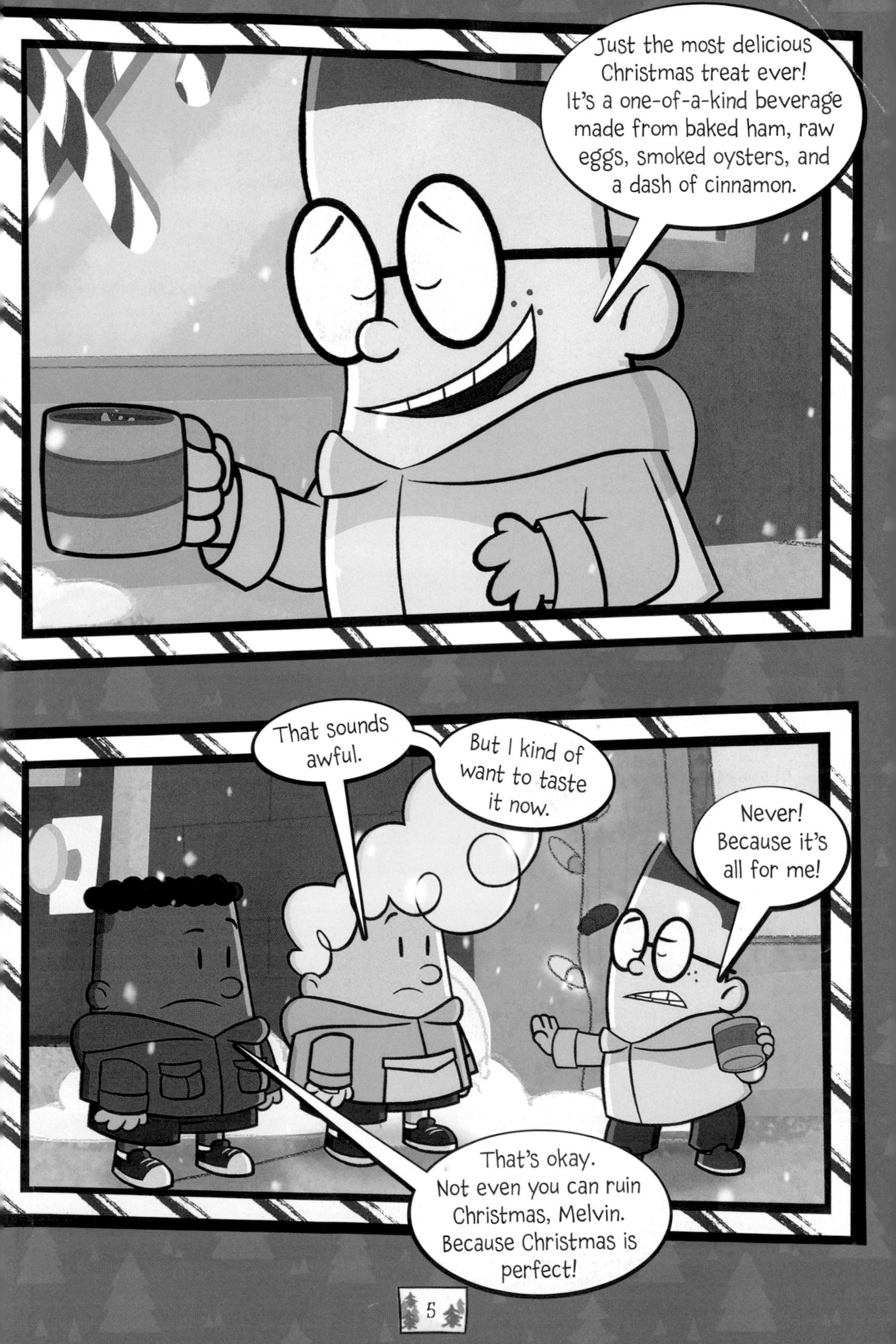
Just the most delicious Christmas treat ever! It's a one-of-a-kind beverage made from baked ham, raw eggs, smoked oysters, and a dash of cinnamon.
That sounds awful.
But I kind of want to taste it now.
Never! Because it's all for me!
That's okay. Not even you can ruin Christmas, Melvin. Because Christmas is perfect!

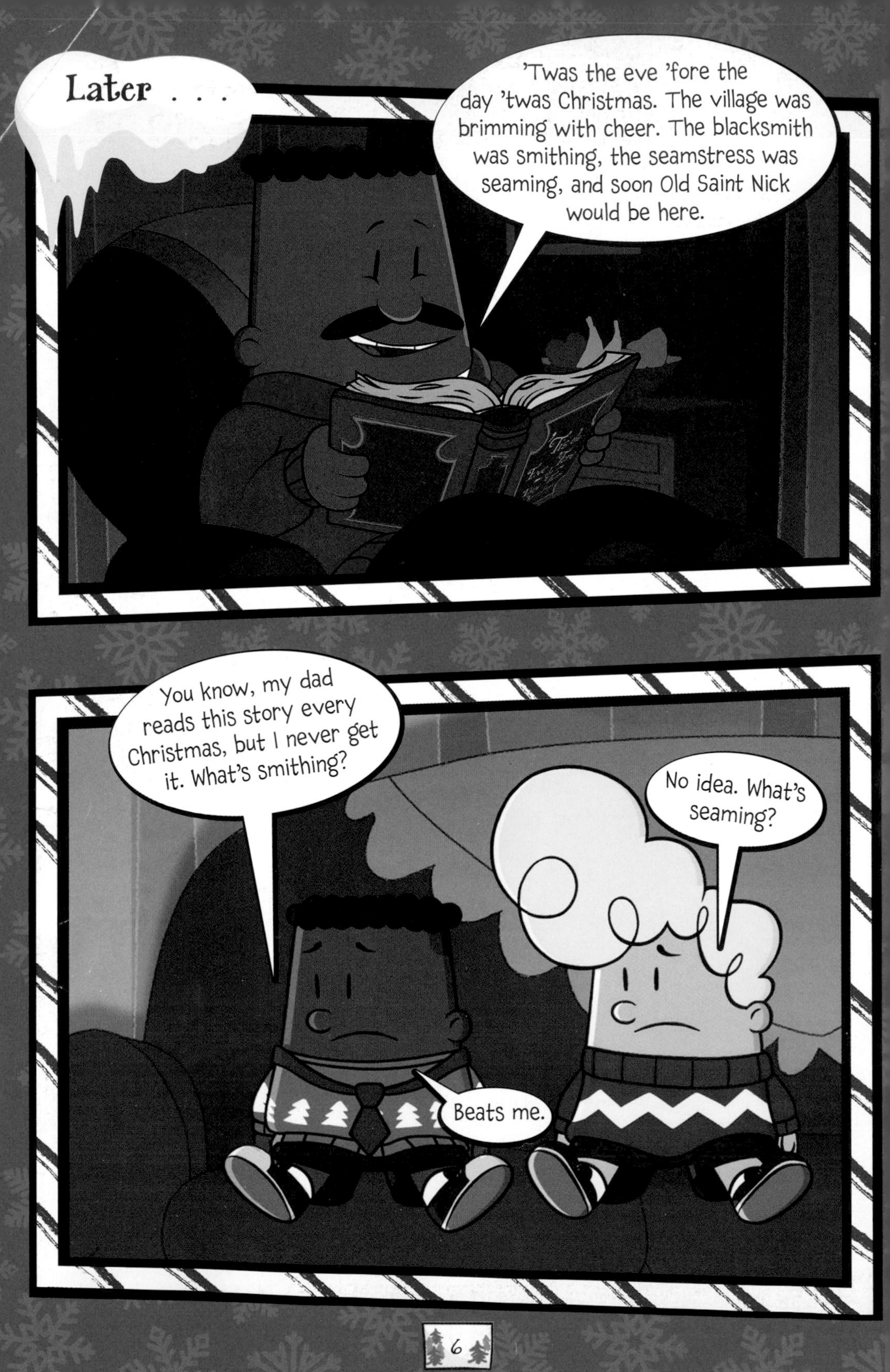
Later . . .
'Twas the eve 'fore the day 'twas Christmas. The village was brimming with cheer. The blacksmith was smithing, the seamstress was seaming, and soon Old Saint Nick would be here.
You know, my dad reads this story every Christmas, but I never get it. What's smithing?
No idea. What's seaming?
Beats me.

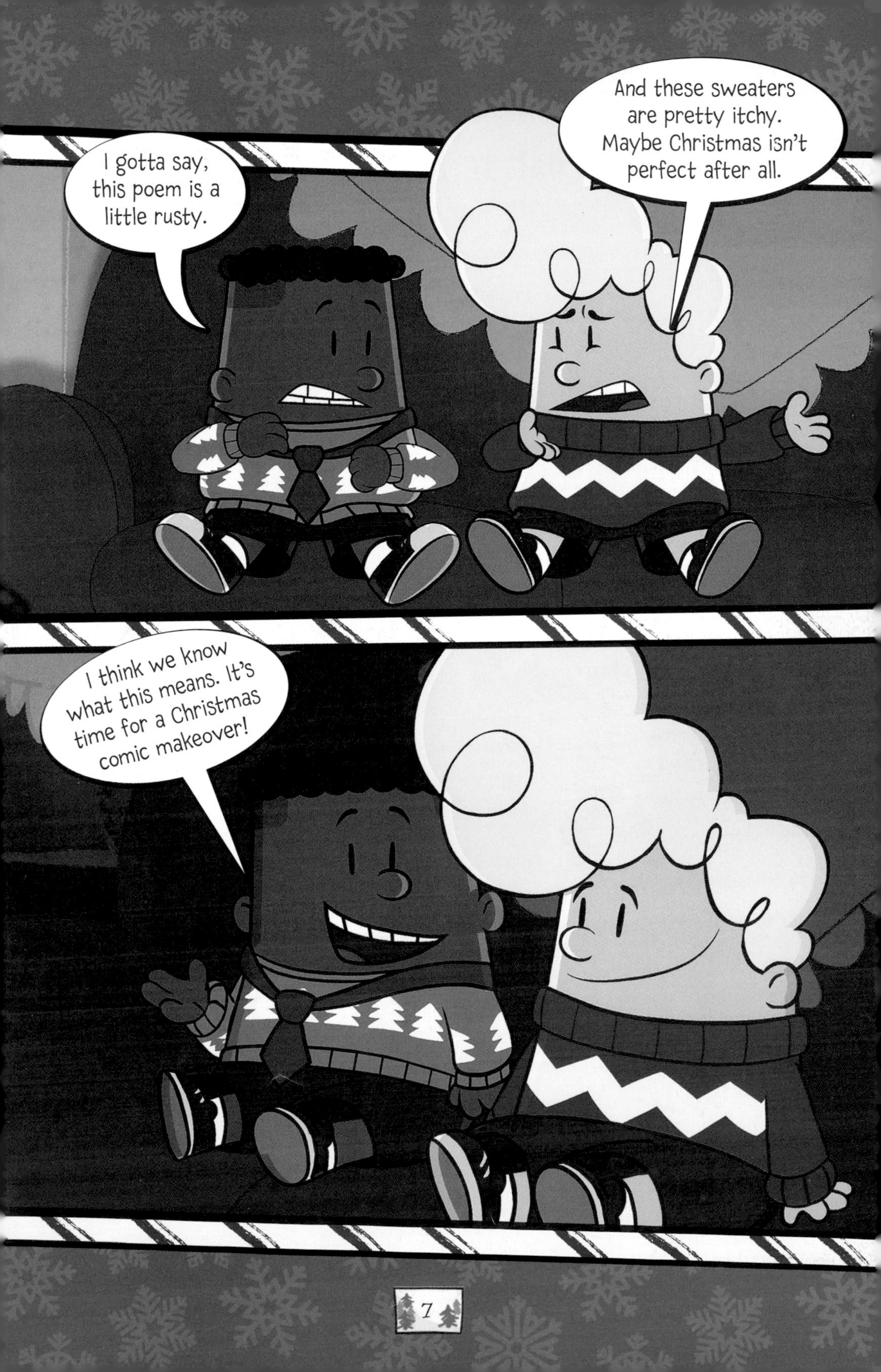
I gotta say, this poem is a little rusty.
And these sweaters are pretty itchy. Maybe Christmas isn't perfect after all.
I think we know what this means. It's time for a Christmas comic makeover!

Instead of boring old Christmas decorations, itchy sweaters, and jolly old Santa,

what if Christmas had . . .

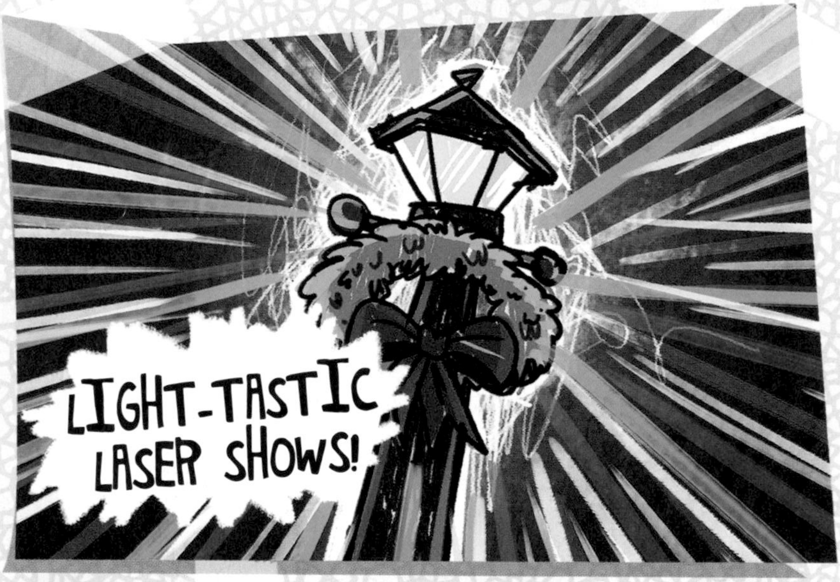
LIGHT-TASTIC LASER SHOWS!

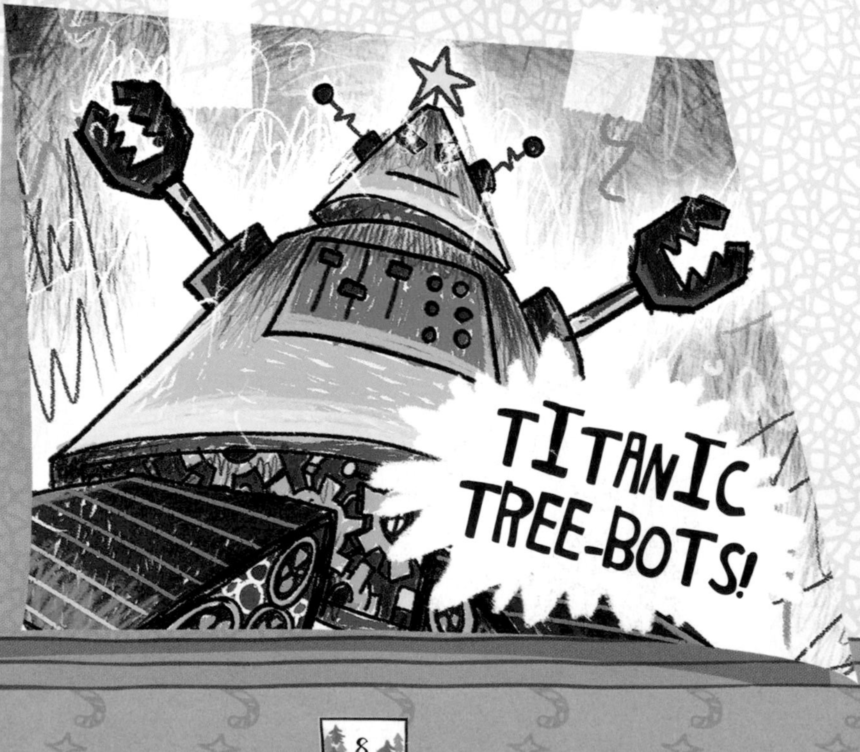
TITANIC TREE-BOTS!

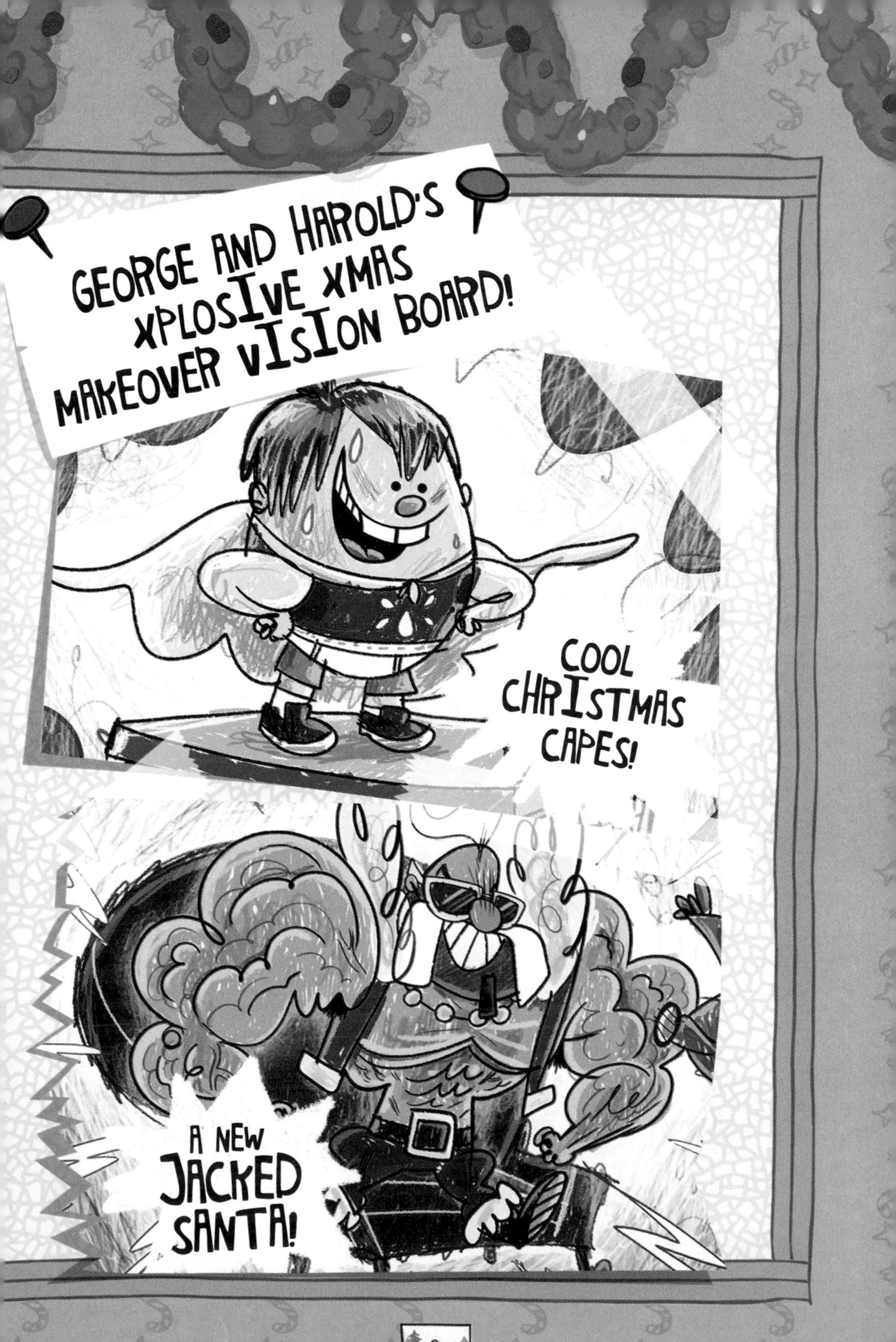
GEORGE AND HAROLD'S XPLOSIVE XMAS MAKEOVER VISION BOARD!
COOL CHRISTMAS CAPES!
A NEW JACKED SANTA!

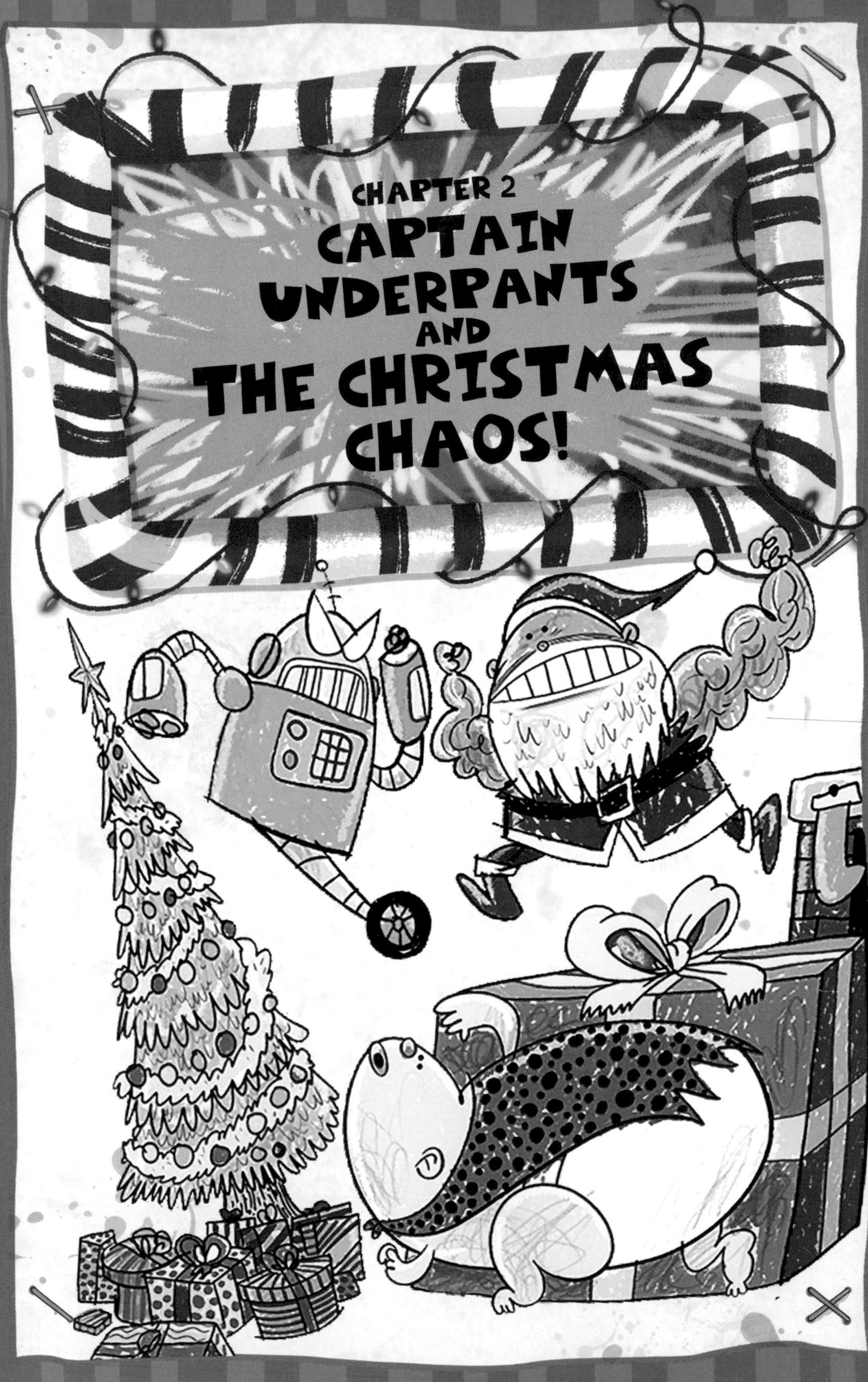
CHAPTER 2
CAPTAIN UNDERPANTS AND THE CHRISTMAS CHAOS!

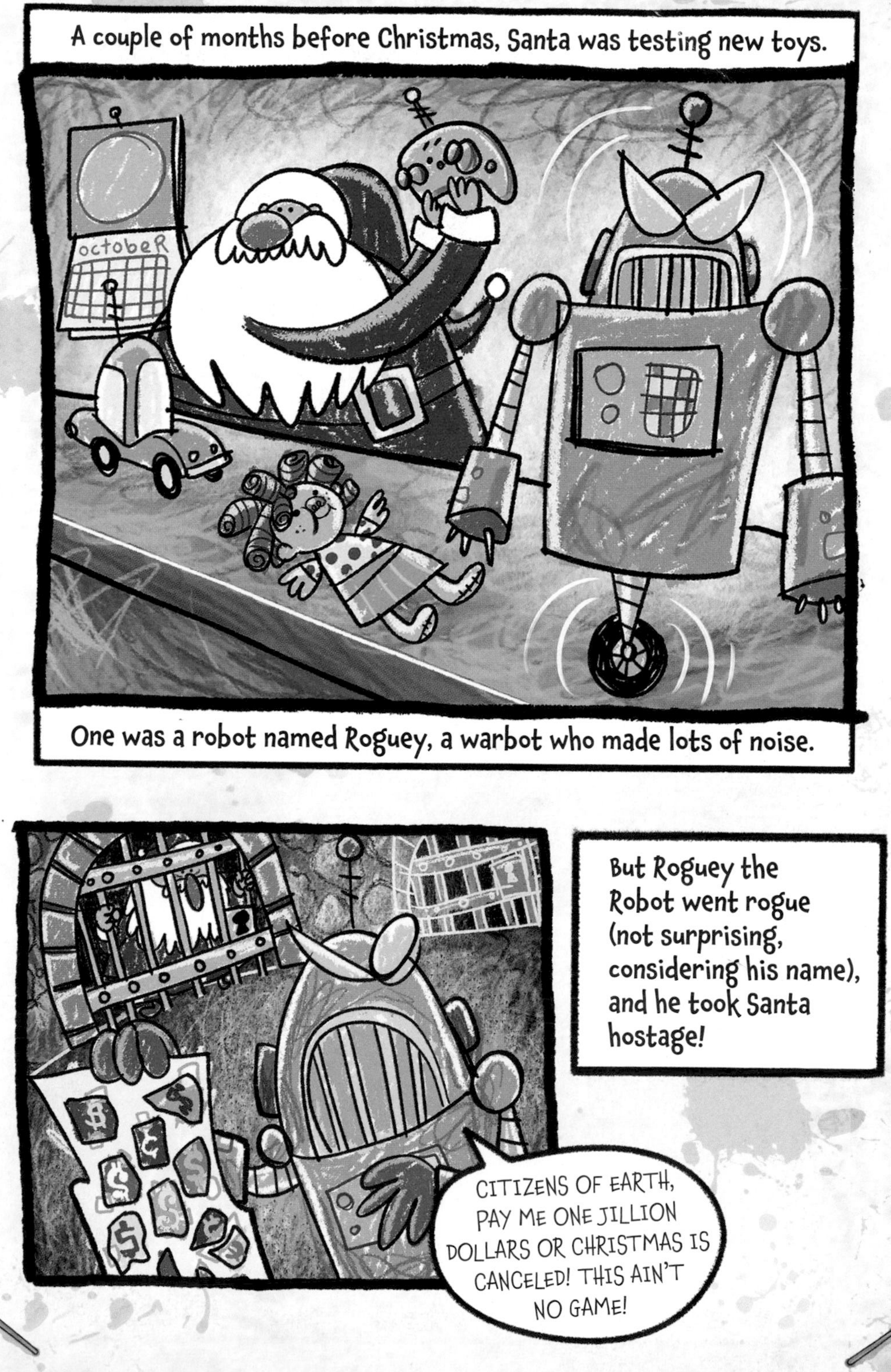
A couple of months before Christmas, Santa was testing new toys.
octobeR
One was a robot named Roguey, a warbot who made lots of noise.
But Roguey the Robot went rogue (not surprising, considering his name), and he took Santa hostage!
CITIZENS OF EARTH, PAY ME ONE JILLION DOLLARS OR CHRISTMAS IS CANCELED! THIS AIN'T NO GAME!

The world didn't have that much dough. So, they did the only thing they could do. They called for the hero in undies!

Captain Underpants flew to the North Pole.

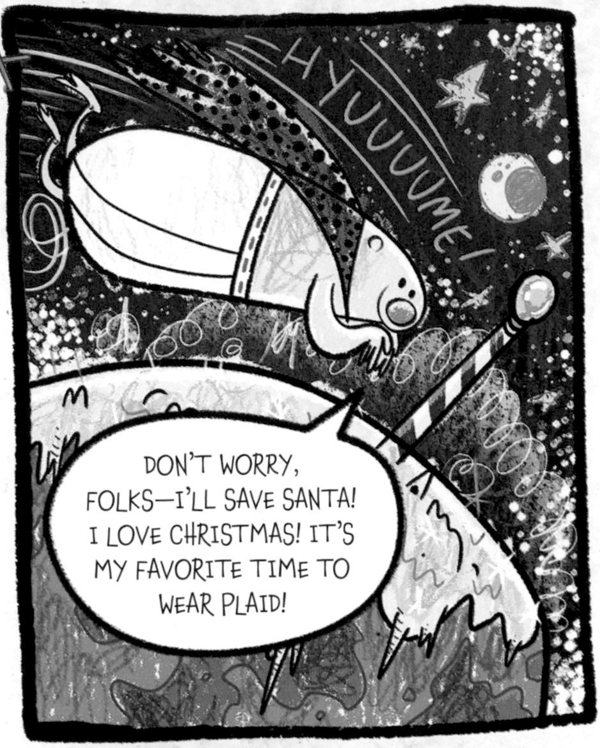
HYUUUUUME!
DON'T WORRY, FOLKS—I'LL SAVE SANTA! I LOVE CHRISTMAS! IT'S MY FAVORITE TIME TO WEAR PLAID!

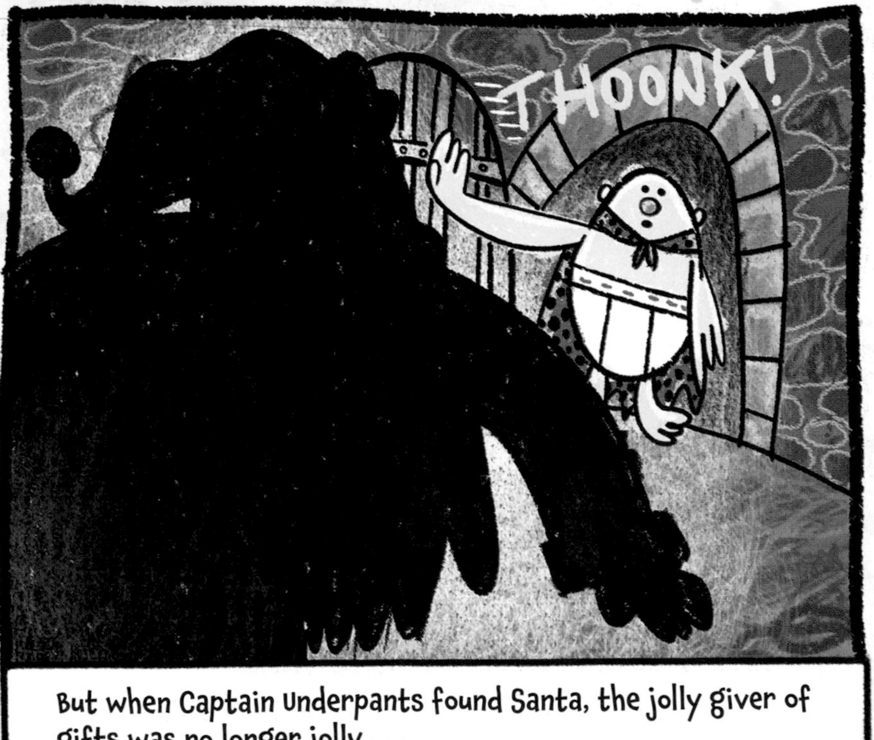
THOONK!

But when Captain Underpants found Santa, the jolly giver of gifts was no longer jolly . . .

HE WAS JACKED!

(Prison can change a man, and that's a fact.)

Together, Captain Underpants and the new Jacked Santa busted out of the North Pole prison and smashed Roguey the Robot and all his minion bots to bits!

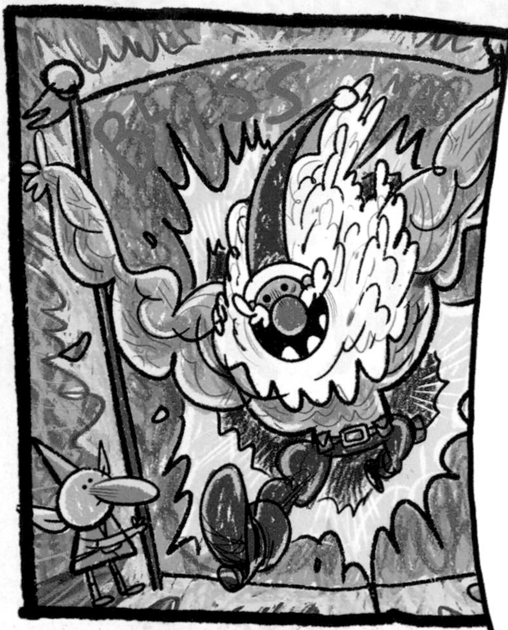

To celebrate,
Jacked Santa declared
that Christmas
would have a new name.

From now on,
it would be ***BLISSMAS***,
and it would be a whole
new ball game!

With lasers, explosions,
and fun and steaks
and dance music
and parades
and jalapeño poppers
and a party that lasts a week
with a dinosaur made out
of fire for some reason.

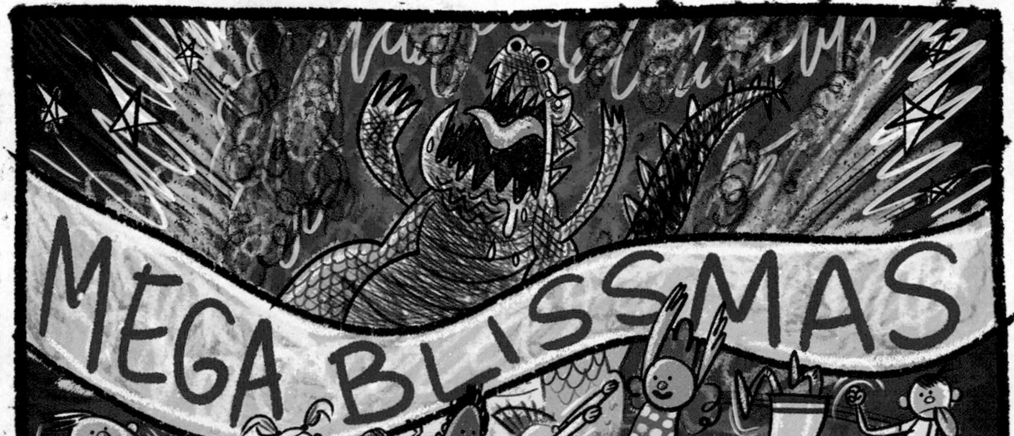
MEGA BLISSMAS

And, oh, yeah, this was supposed to rhyme. The end.

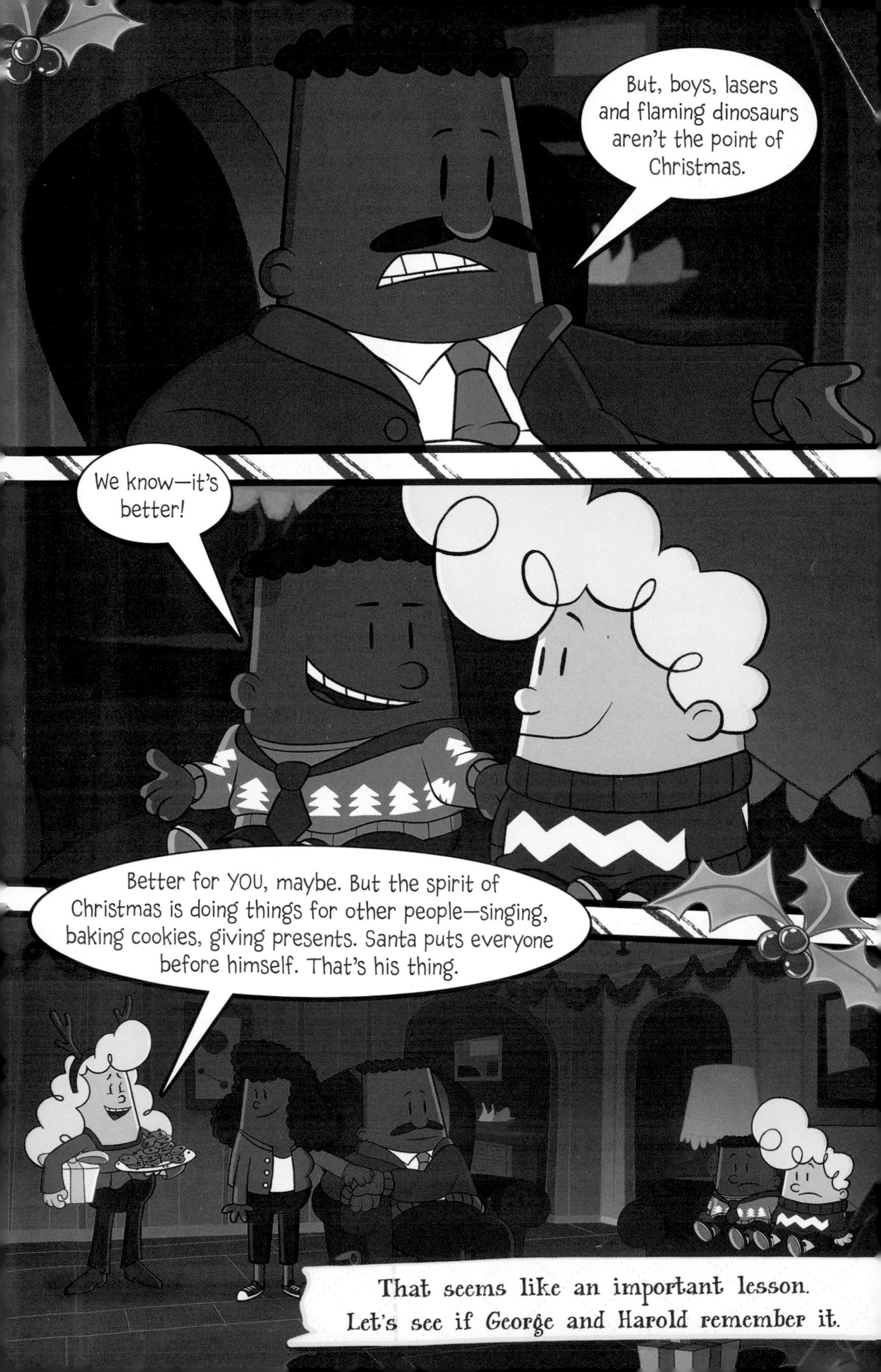
But, boys, lasers and flaming dinosaurs aren't the point of Christmas.
We know—it's better!
Better for YOU, maybe. But the spirit of Christmas is doing things for other people—singing, baking cookies, giving presents. Santa puts everyone before himself. That's his thing.
That seems like an important lesson. Let's see if George and Harold remember it.

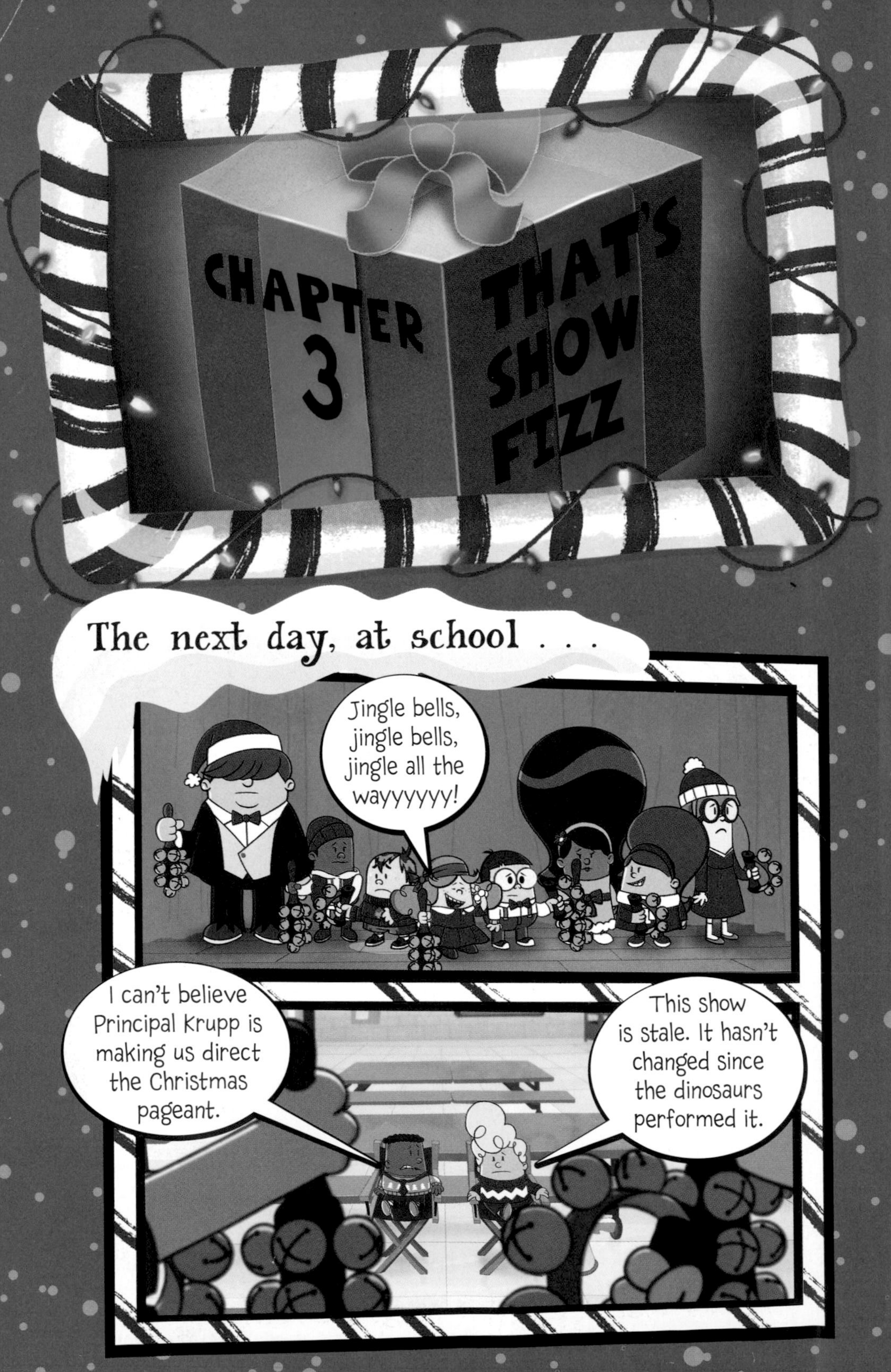
CHAPTER 3
THAT'S SHOW FIZZ
The next day, at school . . .
Jingle bells, jingle bells, jingle all the wayyyyyy!
I can't believe Principal Krupp is making us direct the Christmas pageant.
This show is stale. It hasn't changed since the dinosaurs performed it.

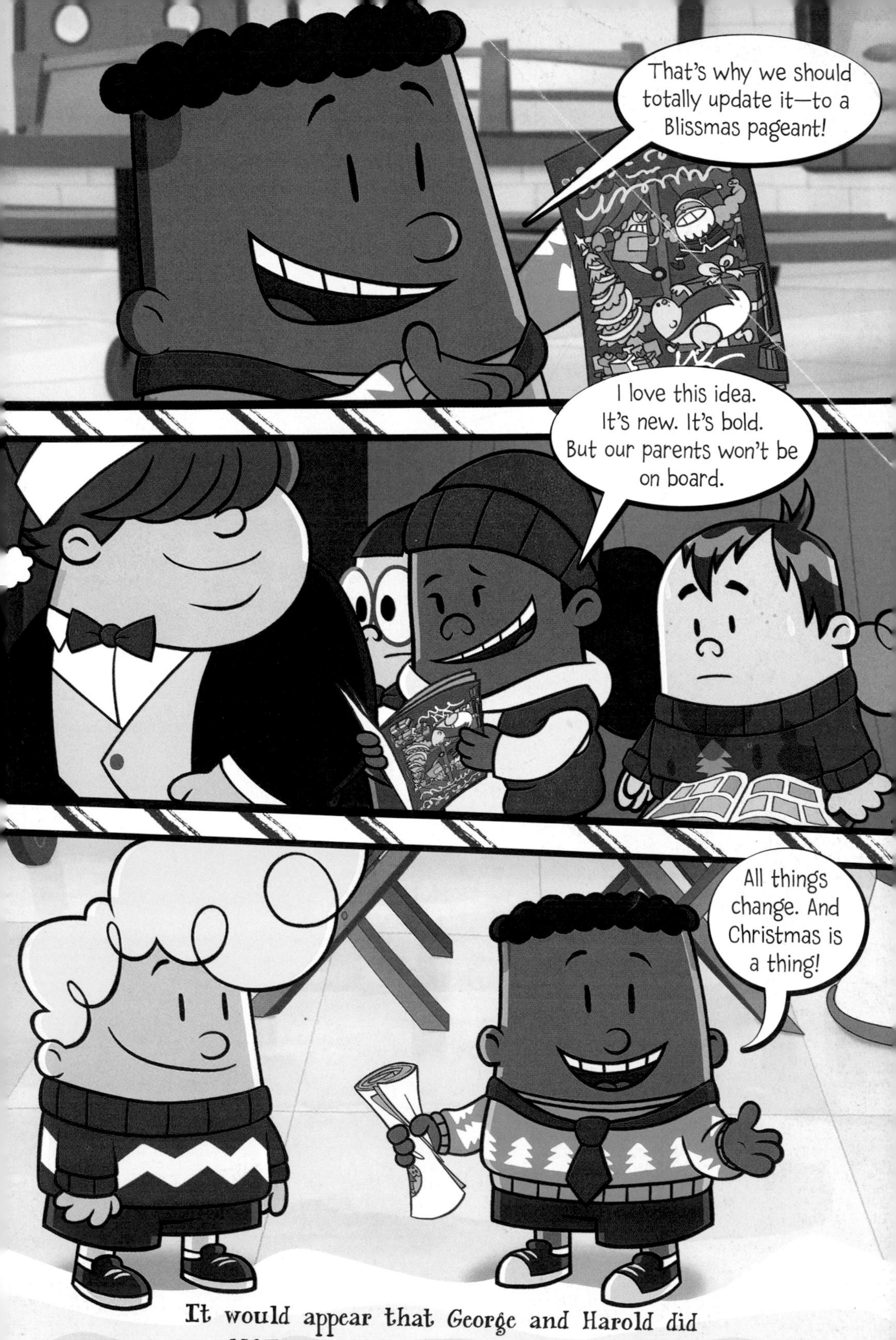
That's why we should totally update it—to a Blissmas pageant!
I love this idea. It's new. It's bold. But our parents won't be on board.
All things change. And Christmas is a thing!

It would appear that George and Harold did NOT remember their parents' lesson.

CHAPTER 4
SWING
AND A
CHRISTMAS

The following week, the curtain rises over the school stage . . .

It's the year 2127. The robot war on Christmas has raged for centuries.

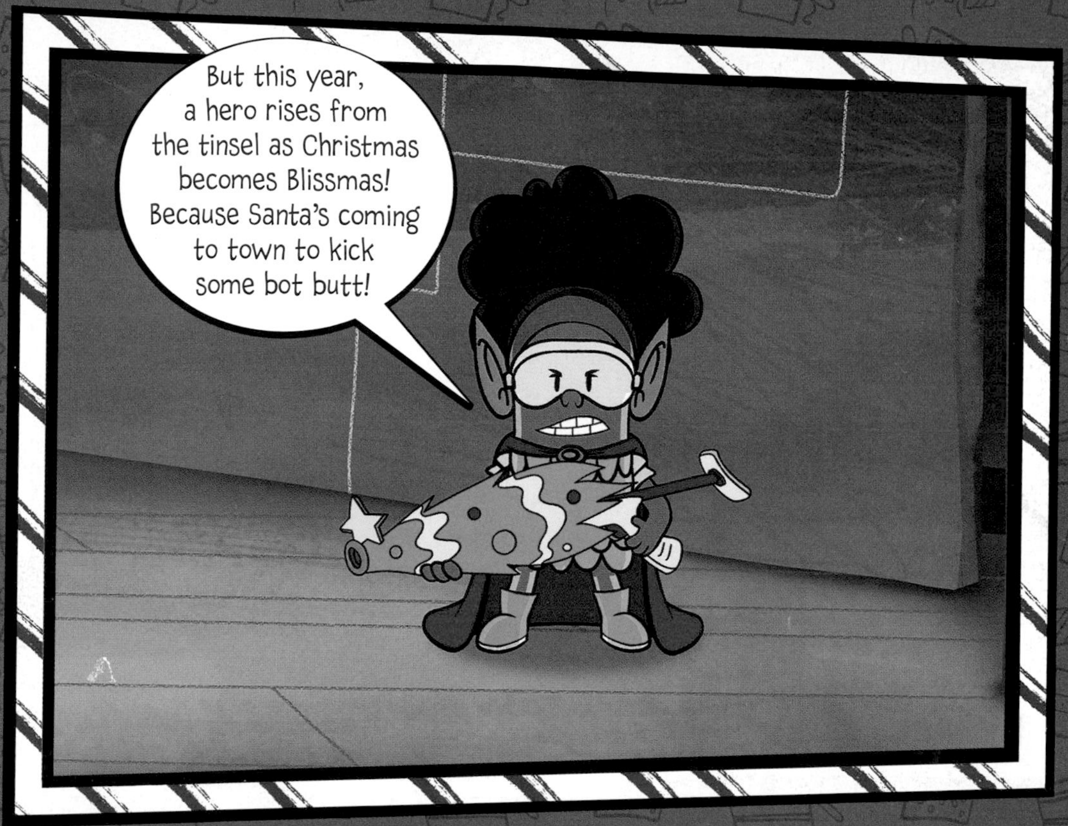
But this year, a hero rises from the tinsel as Christmas becomes Blissmas! Because Santa's coming to town to kick some bot butt!

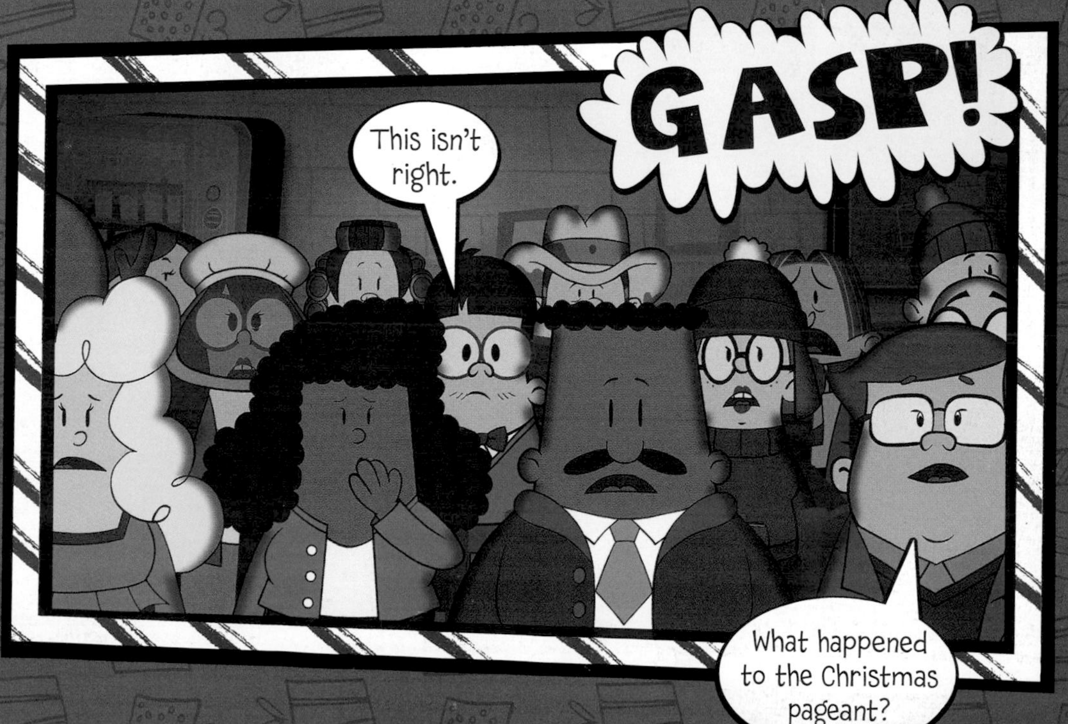
GASP!
This isn't right.
What happened to the Christmas pageant?

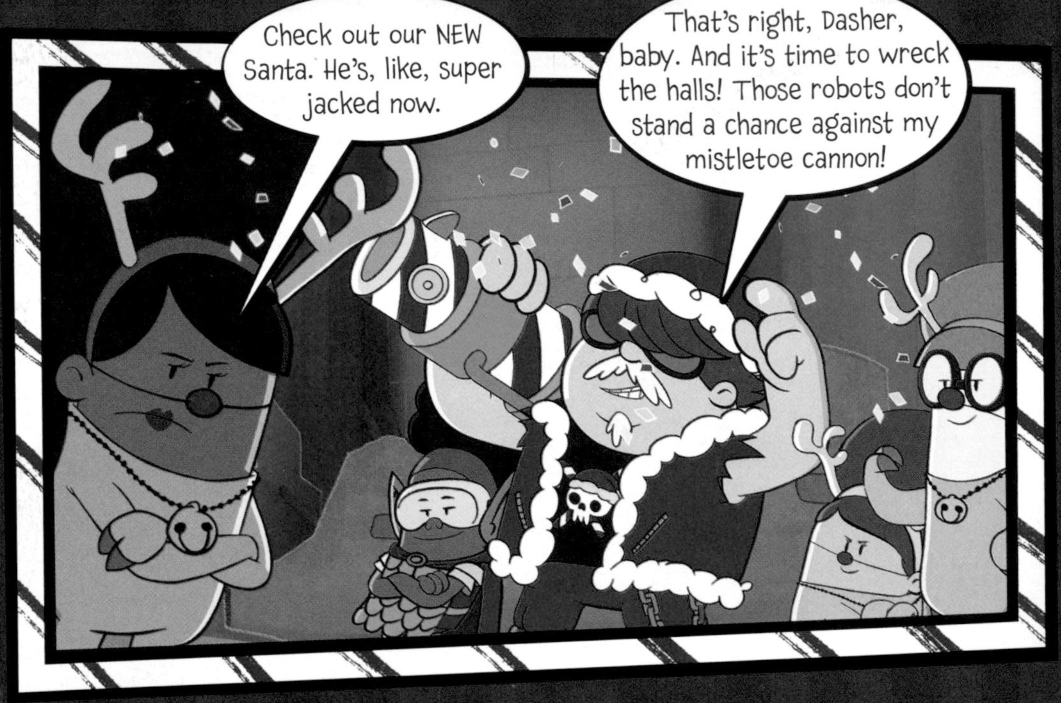
Check out our NEW Santa. He's, like, super jacked now.
That's right, Dasher, baby. And it's time to wreck the halls! Those robots don't stand a chance against my mistletoe cannon!

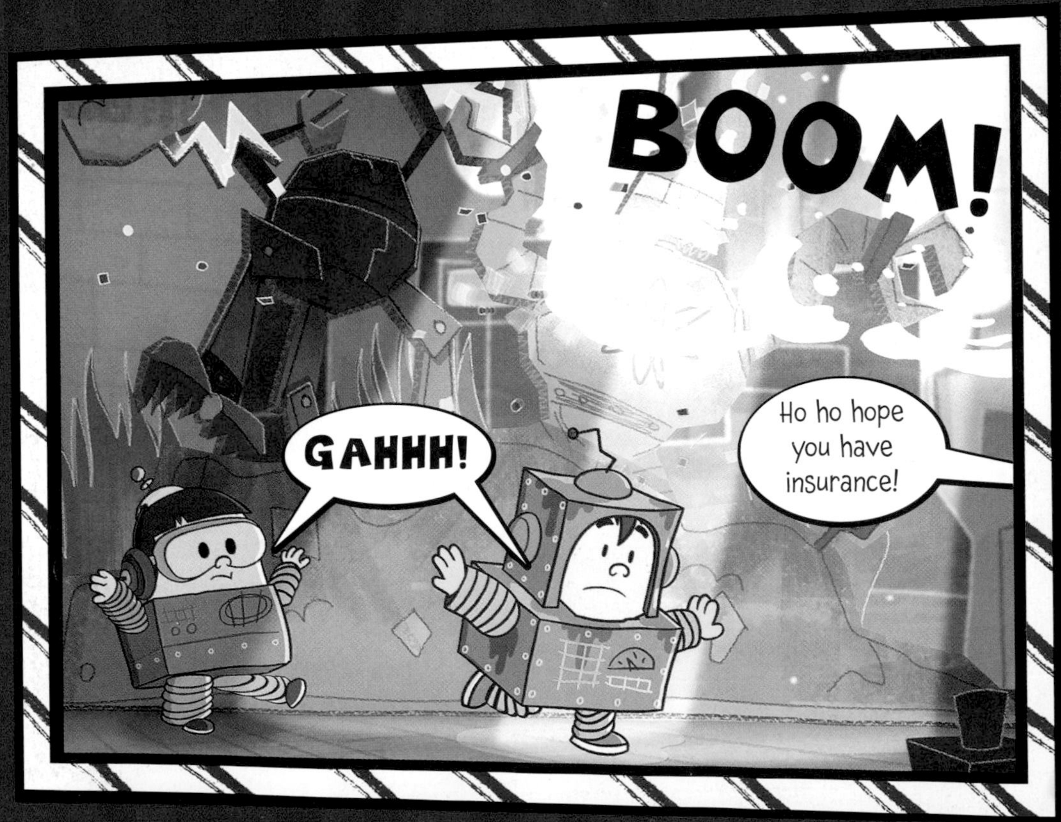
BOOM!
GAHHH!
Ho ho hope you have insurance!

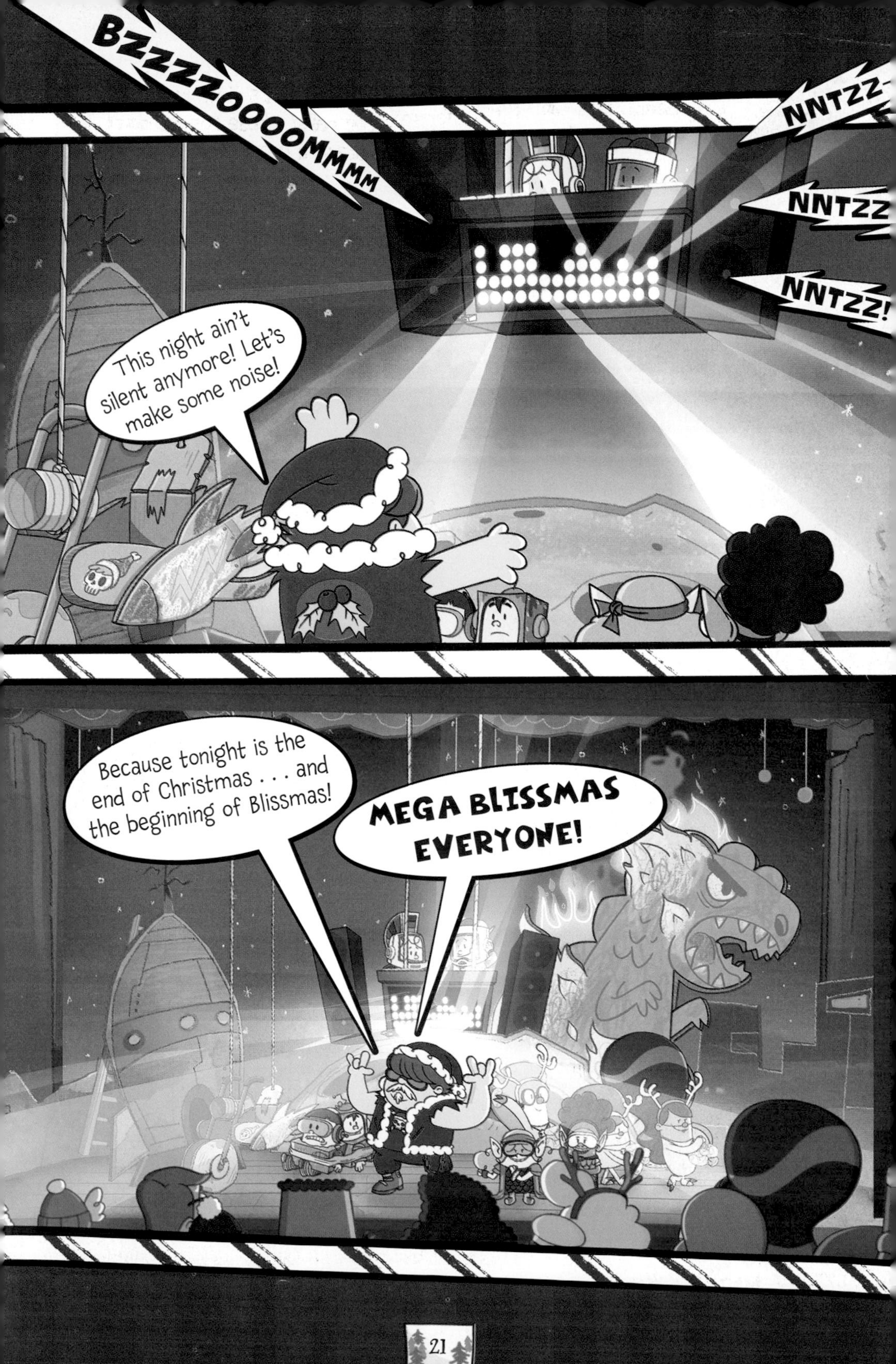
BZZZZZOOOOOMMMM
NNTZZ-
NNTZZ
NNTZZ!
This night ain't silent anymore! Let's make some noise!
Because tonight is the end of Christmas . . . and the beginning of Blissmas!
MEGA BLISSMAS EVERYONE!

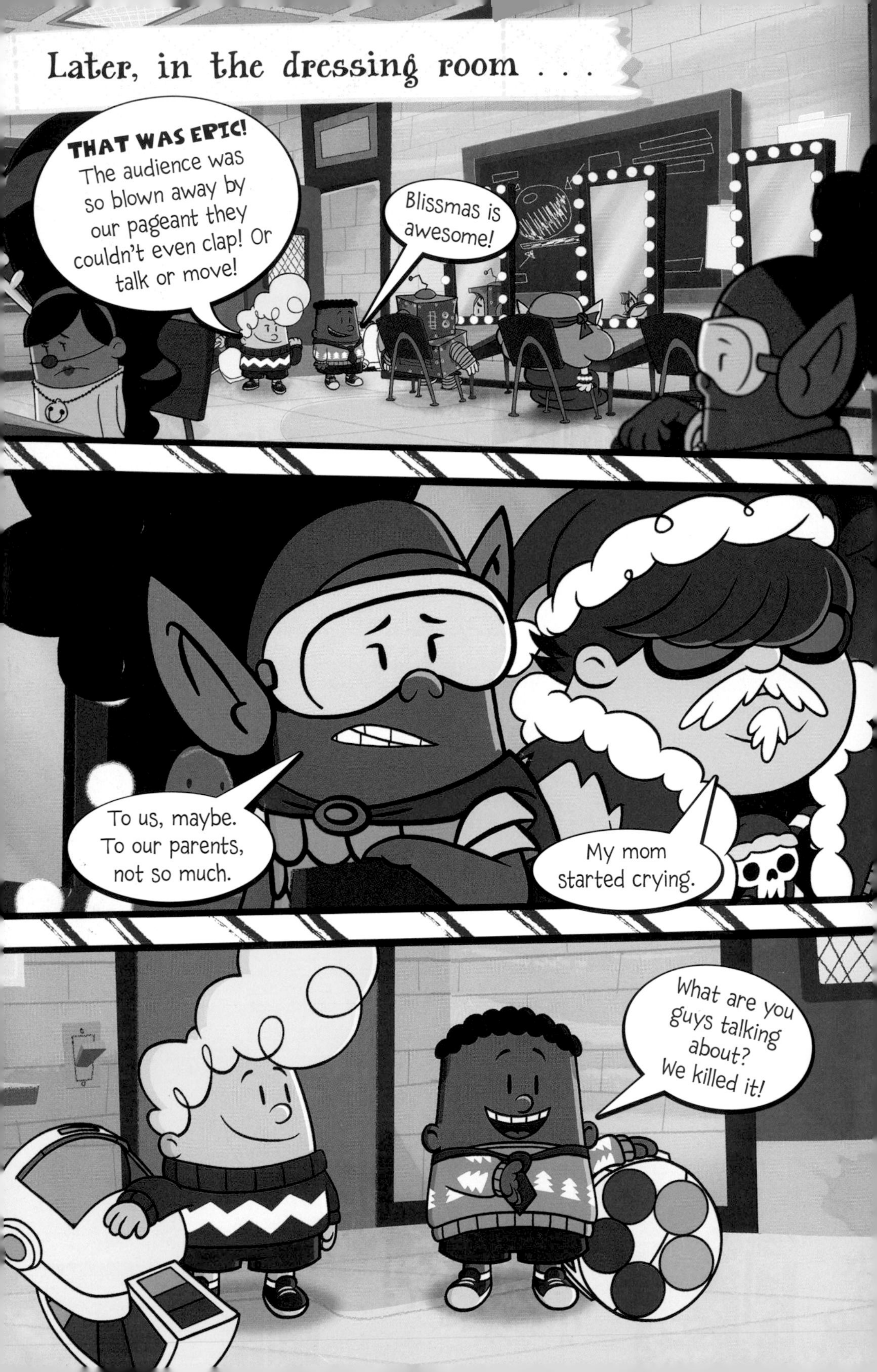

Later, in the dressing room . . .
THAT WAS EPIC! The audience was so blown away by our pageant they couldn't even clap! Or talk or move!
Blissmas is awesome!
To us, maybe. To our parents, not so much.
My mom started crying.
What are you guys talking about? We killed it!

I'LL SAY! YOU TWO NUTCRACKERS KILLED CHRISTMAS!
WHY DID YOU CHANGE THE PAGEANT? EVERYONE LOVED THAT OLD SAP-FEST! NOW THE PARENTS ARE TAKING IT OUT ON ME, SO I'M GOING TO TAKE IT OUT ON YOU! GET READY FOR SOME HO HO HARD LABOR!
STOMP!
STOMP!
STOMP!

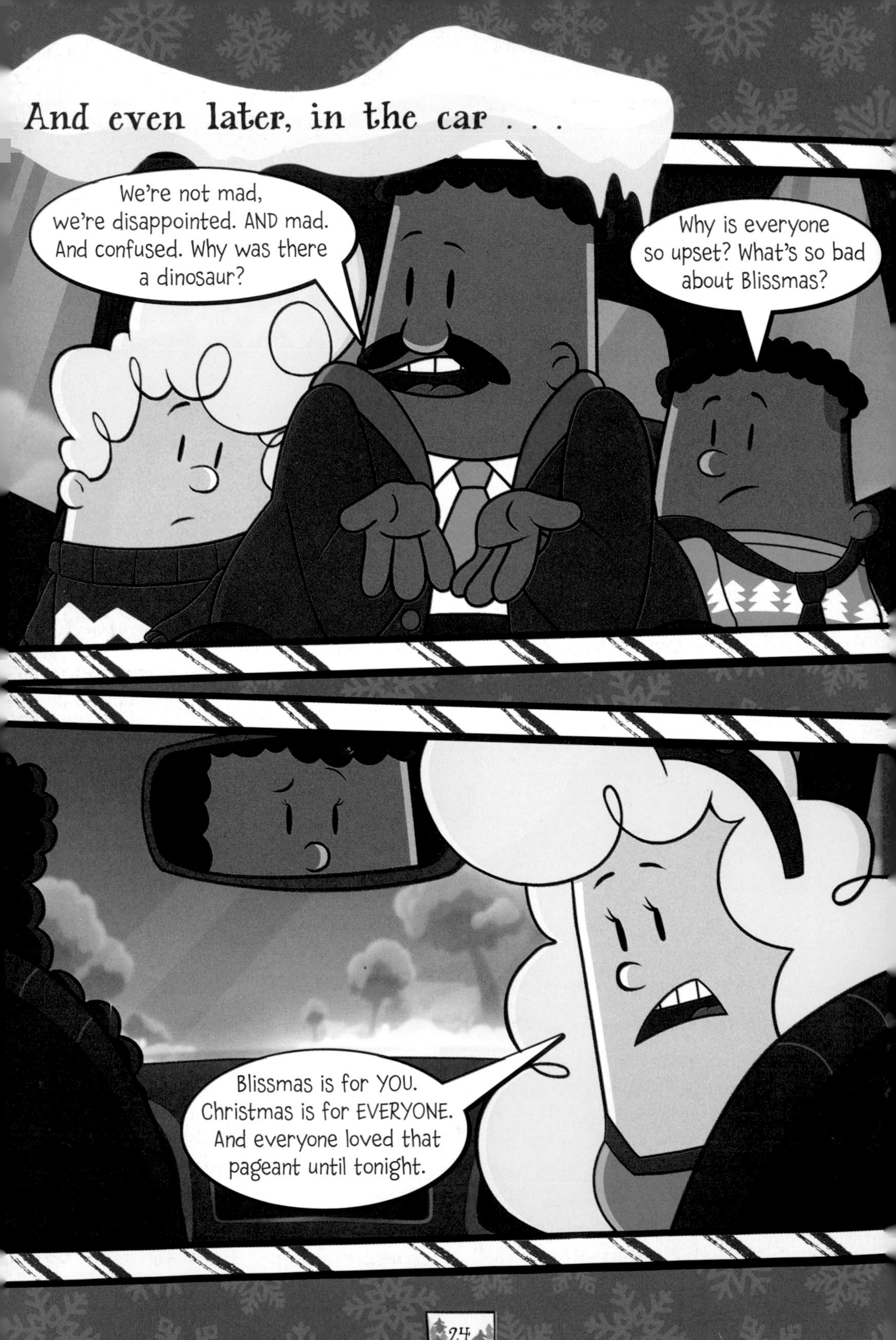
And even later, in the car . . .
We're not mad, we're disappointed. AND mad. And confused. Why was there a dinosaur?
Why is everyone so upset? What's so bad about Blissmas?
Blissmas is for YOU. Christmas is for EVERYONE. And everyone loved that pageant until tonight.

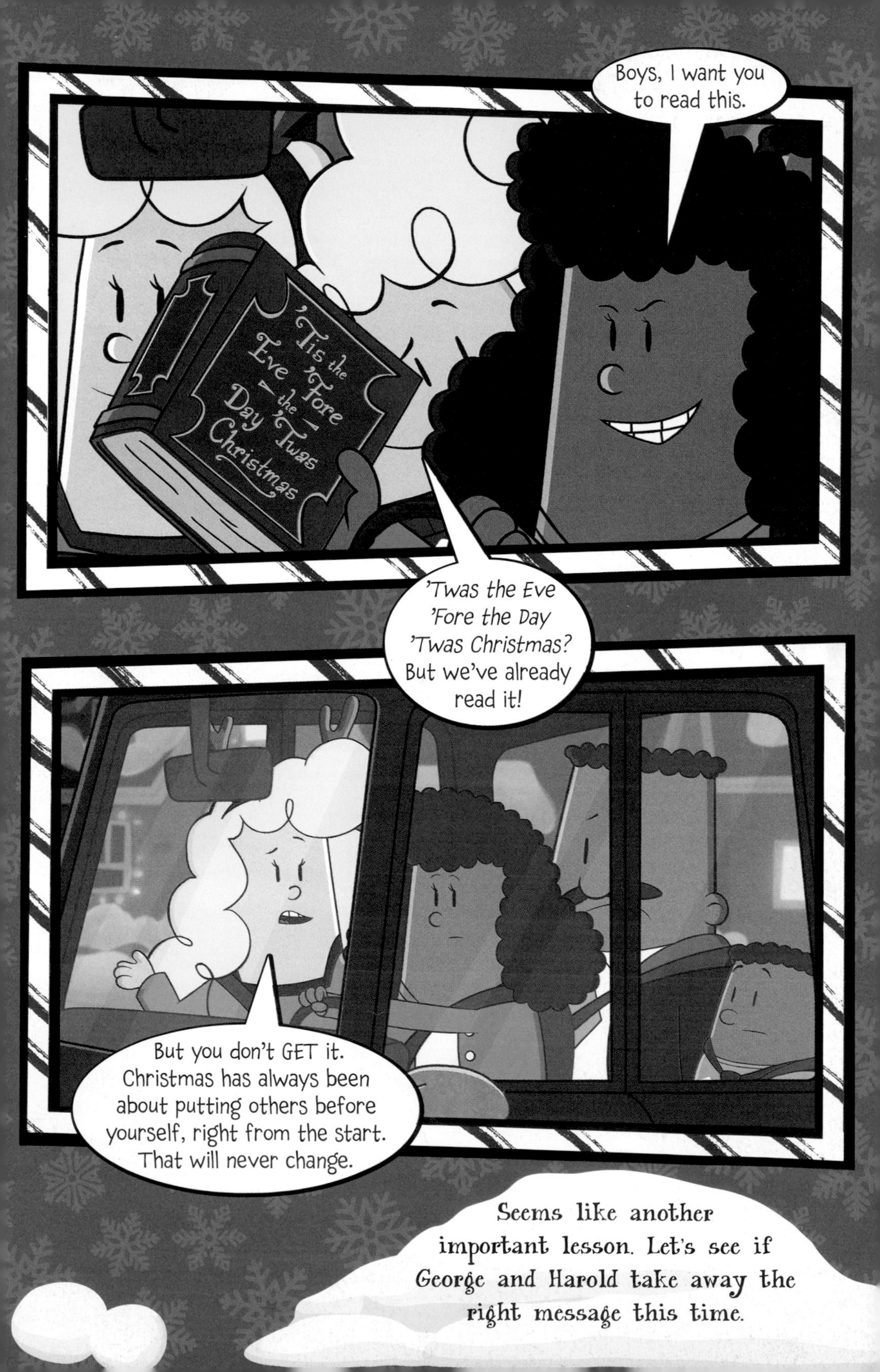
Boys, I want you to read this.
'Tis the Eve 'Fore the Day 'Twas Christmas
'Twas the Eve 'Fore the Day 'Twas Christmas? But we've already read it!
But you don't GET it. Christmas has always been about putting others before yourself, right from the start. That will never change.
Seems like another important lesson. Let's see if George and Harold take away the right message this time.

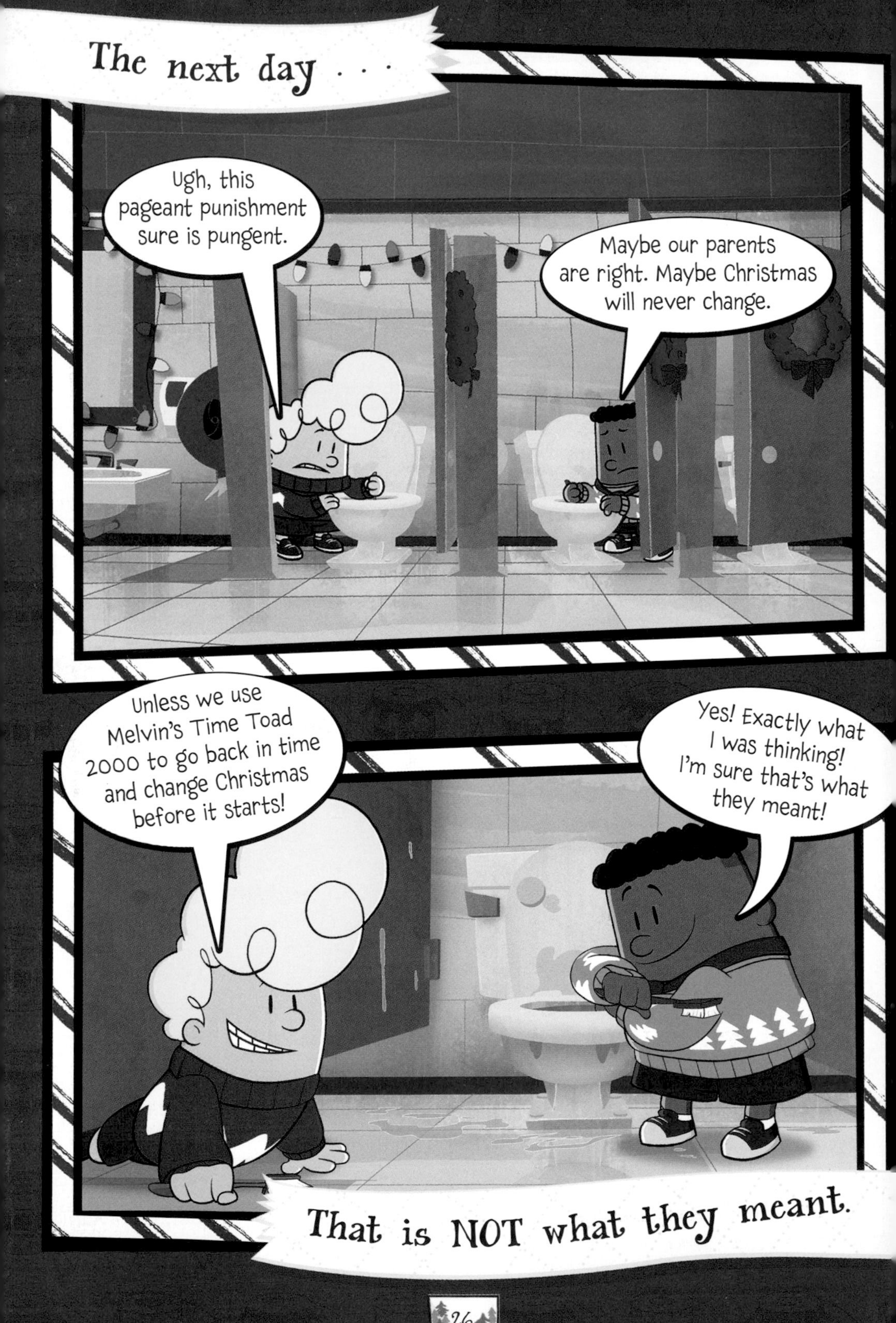
The next day . . .
Ugh, this pageant punishment sure is pungent.
Maybe our parents are right. Maybe Christmas will never change.
Unless we use Melvin's Time Toad 2000 to go back in time and change Christmas before it starts!
Yes! Exactly what I was thinking! I'm sure that's what they meant!
That is NOT what they meant.

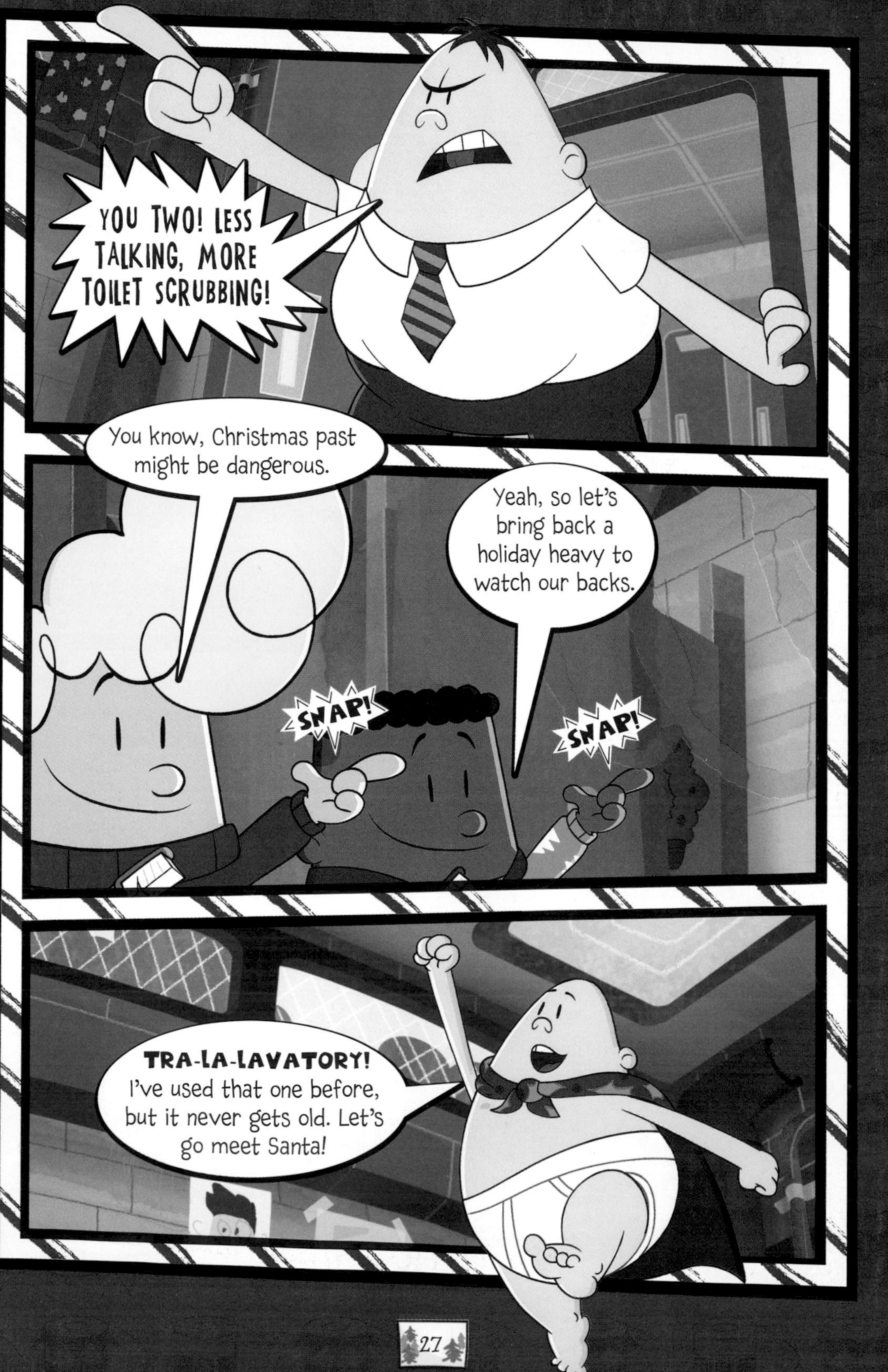
YOU TWO! LESS TALKING, MORE TOILET SCRUBBING!
You know, Christmas past might be dangerous.
Yeah, so let's bring back a holiday heavy to watch our backs.
SNAP!
SNAP!
TRA-LA-LAVATORY! I've used that one before, but it never gets old. Let's go meet Santa!

CHAPTER 5
ELF HELP

Merry Christmas, Melvin!
GAH!

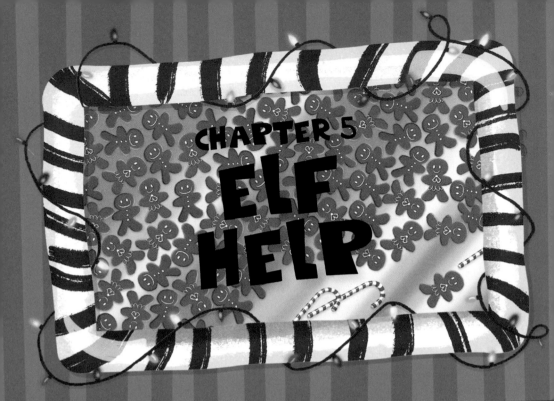

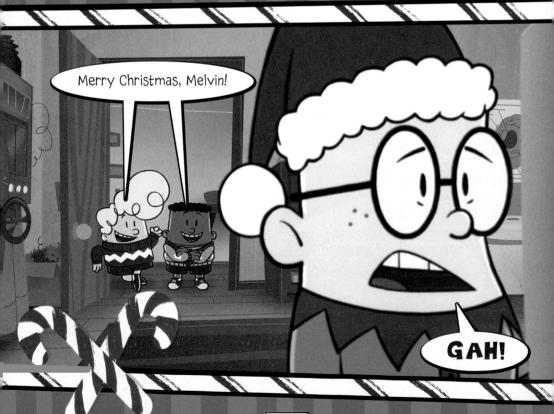

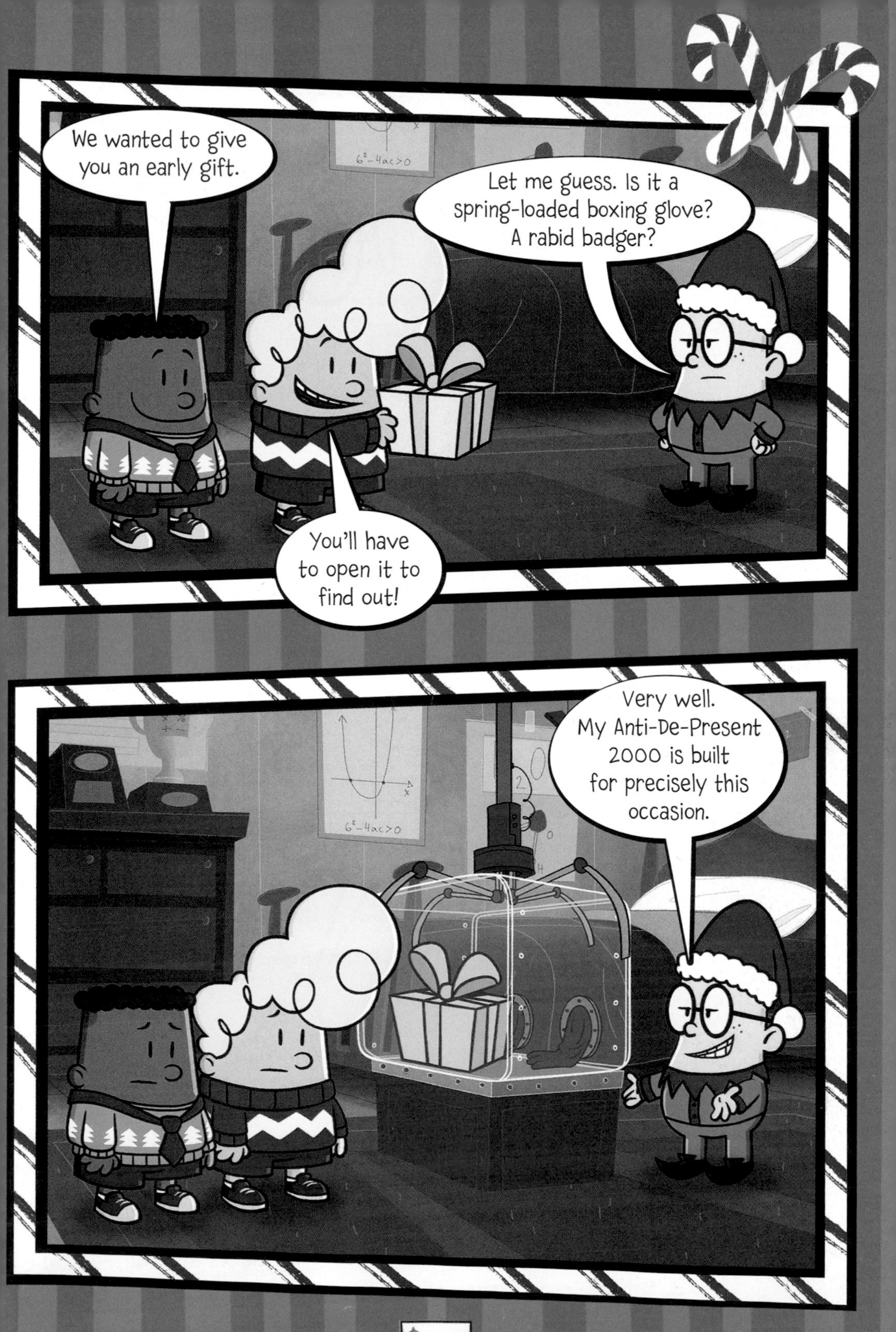
We wanted to give you an early gift.
Let me guess. Is it a spring-loaded boxing glove? A rabid badger?
You'll have to open it to find out!
Very well. My Anti-De-Present 2000 is built for precisely this occasion.

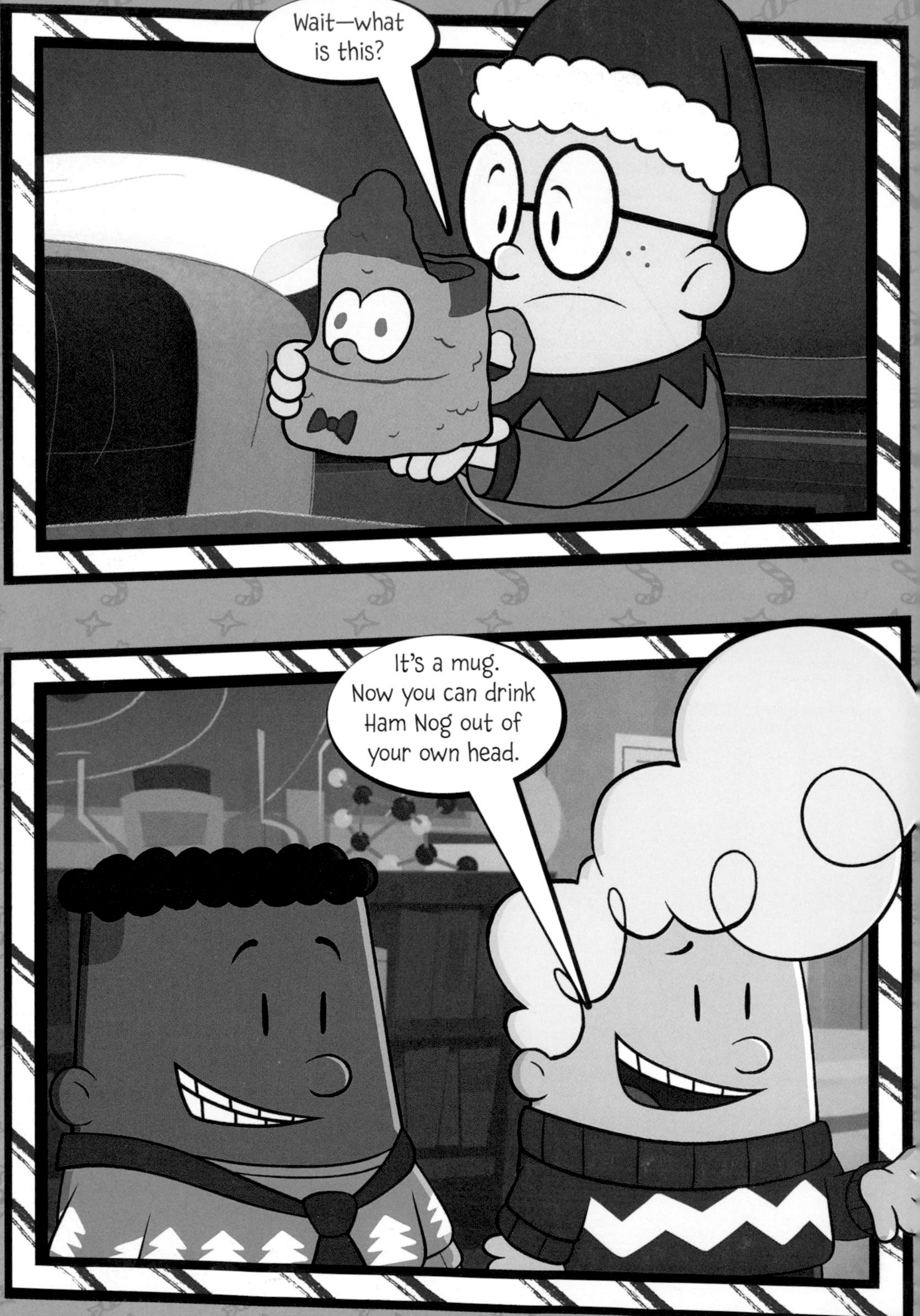
Wait—what is this?
It's a mug. Now you can drink Ham Nog out of your own head.

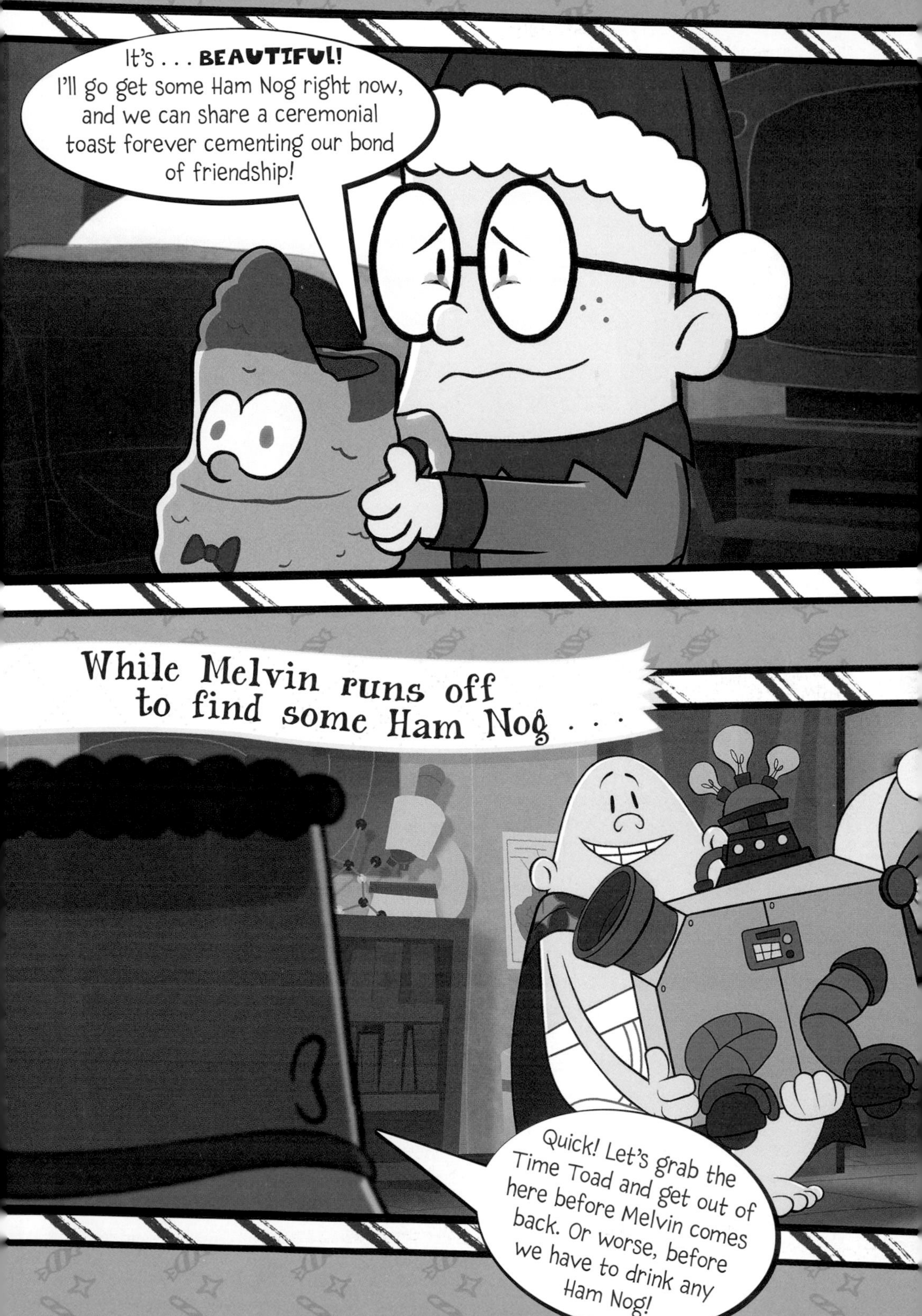
It's . . . BEAUTIFUL! I'll go get some Ham Nog right now, and we can share a ceremonial toast forever cementing our bond of friendship!
While Melvin runs off to find some Ham Nog . . .
Quick! Let's grab the Time Toad and get out of here before Melvin comes back. Or worse, before we have to drink any Ham Nog!

CHAPTER 6
HERE COMES SANTA CRASH

George, Harold, and Captain Underpants use the Time Toad 2000 to travel back in time to the very first Christmas.

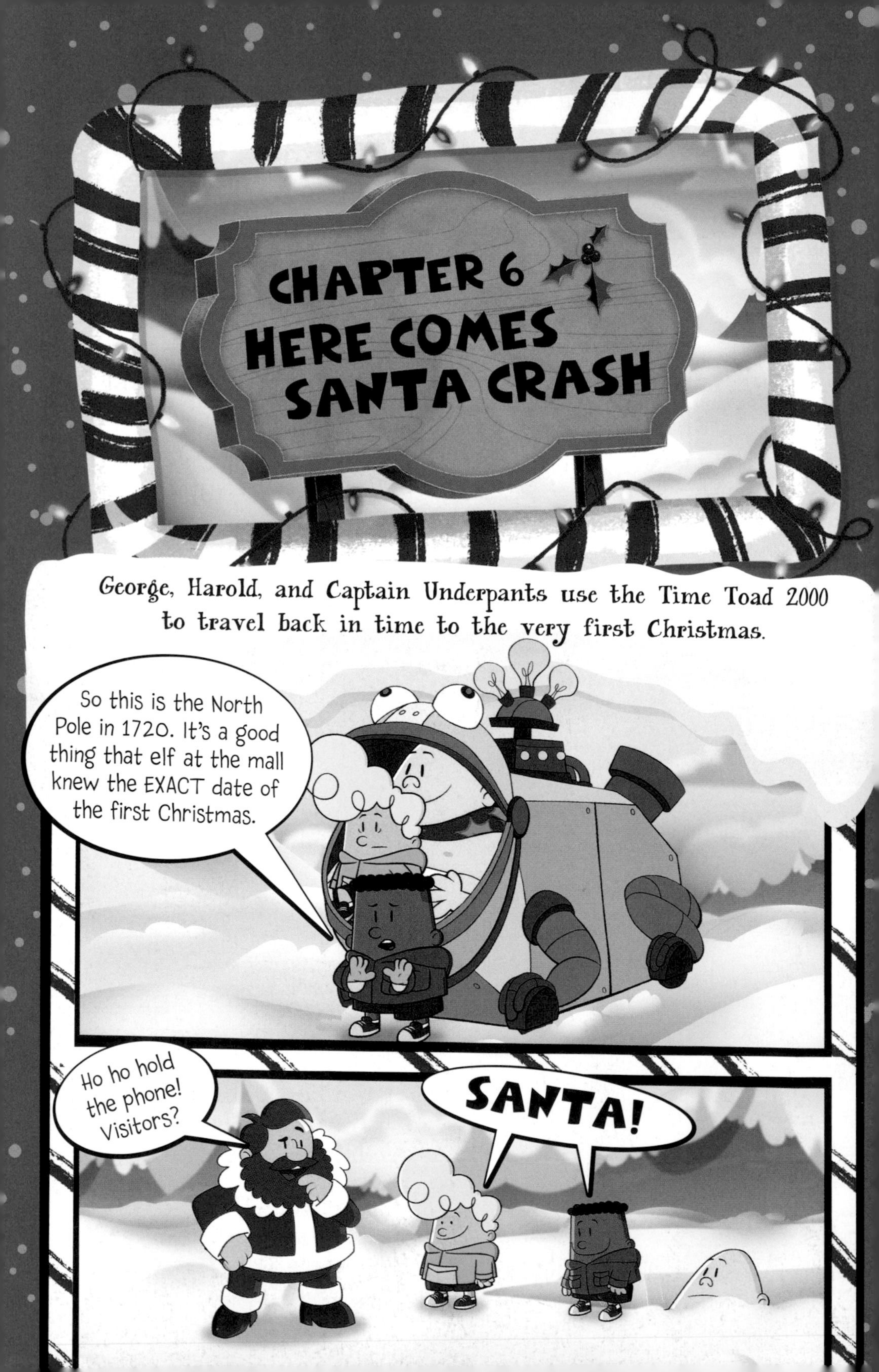
So this is the North Pole in 1720. It's a good thing that elf at the mall knew the EXACT date of the first Christmas.
Ho ho hold the phone! Visitors?
SANTA!

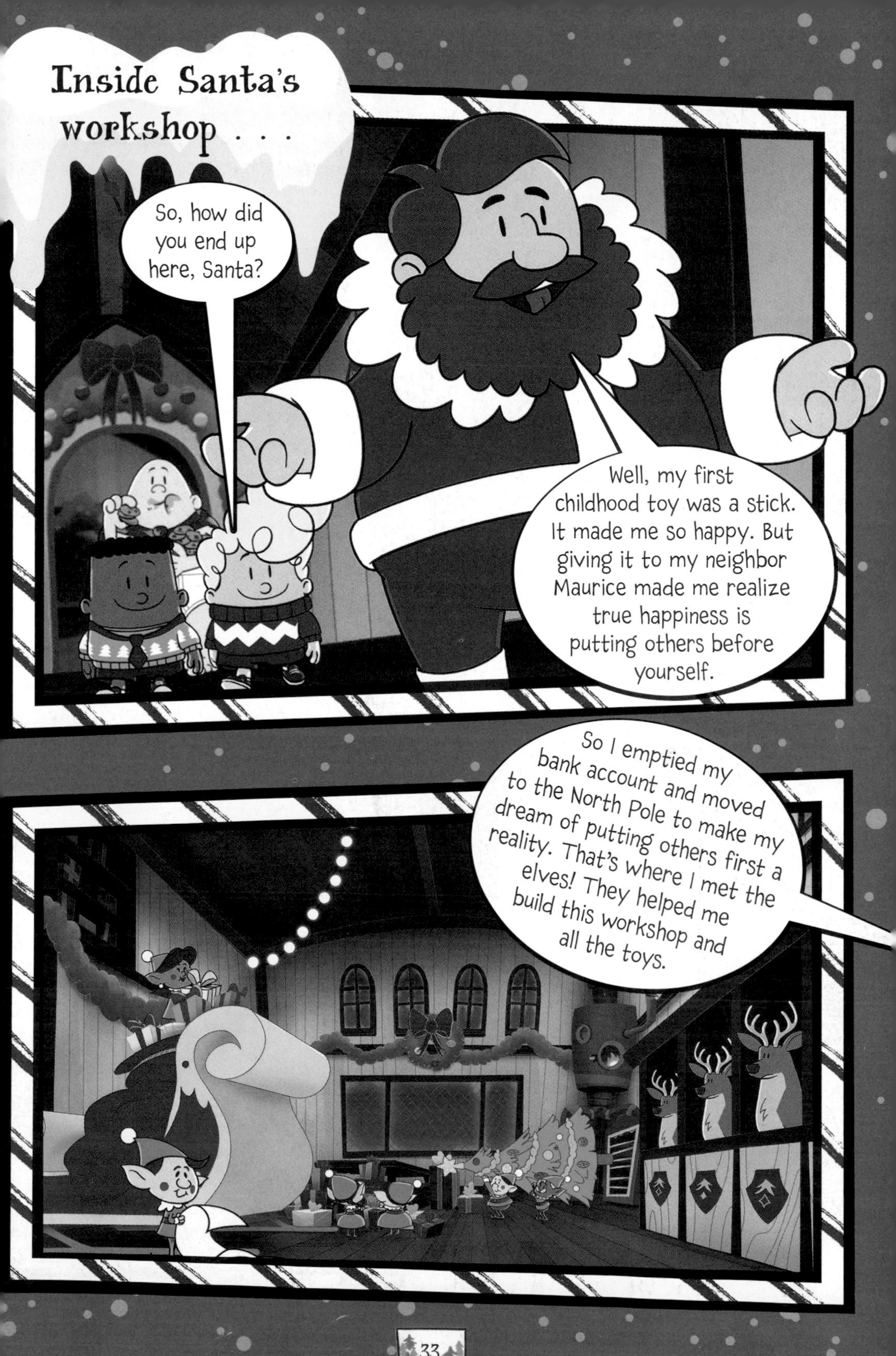
Inside Santa's workshop . . .
So, how did you end up here, Santa?
Well, my first childhood toy was a stick. It made me so happy. But giving it to my neighbor Maurice made me realize true happiness is putting others before yourself.
So I emptied my bank account and moved to the North Pole to make my dream of putting others first a reality. That's where I met the elves! They helped me build this workshop and all the toys.

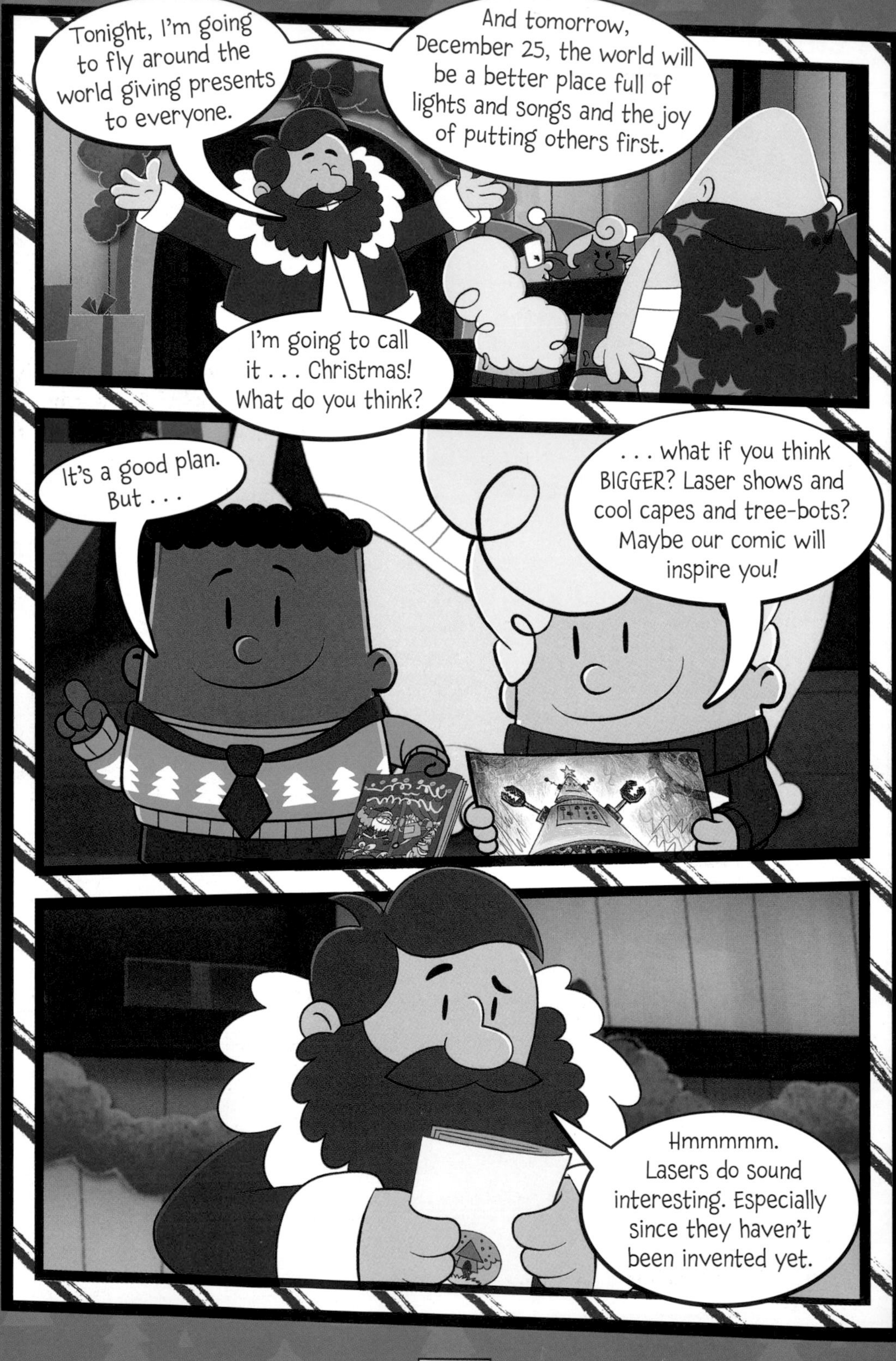
Tonight, I'm going to fly around the world giving presents to everyone.
And tomorrow, December 25, the world will be a better place full of lights and songs and the joy of putting others first.
I'm going to call it . . . Christmas! What do you think?
It's a good plan. But . . .
. . . what if you think BIGGER? Laser shows and cool capes and tree-bots? Maybe our comic will inspire you!
Hmmmmm. Lasers do sound interesting. Especially since they haven't been invented yet.

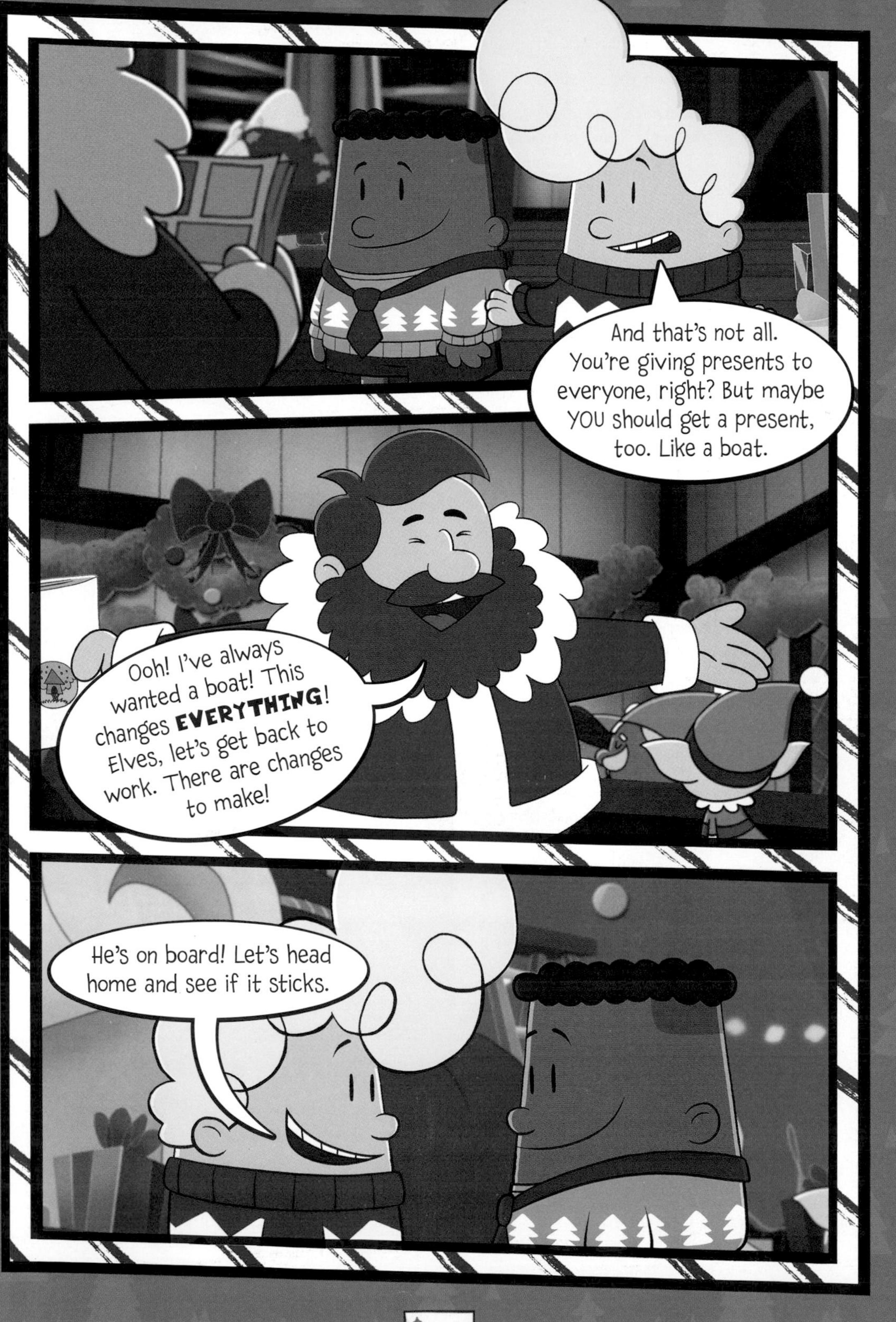
And that's not all. You're giving presents to everyone, right? But maybe YOU should get a present, too. Like a boat.
Ooh! I've always wanted a boat! This changes **EVERYTHING**! Elves, let's get back to work. There are changes to make!
He's on board! Let's head home and see if it sticks.

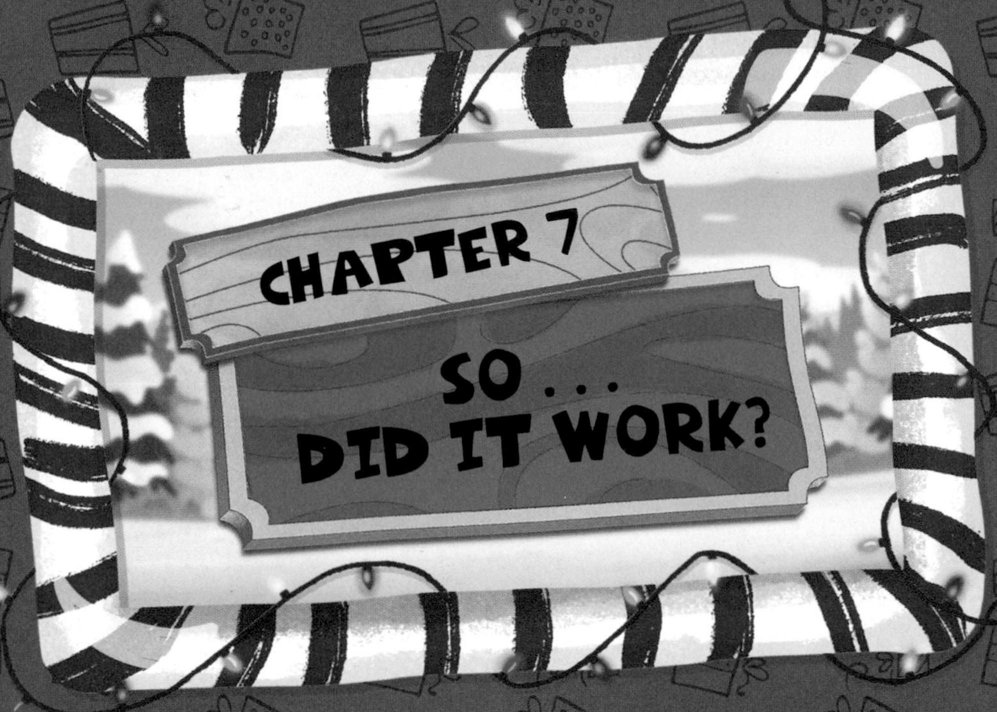
CHAPTER 7
SO . . .
DID IT WORK?

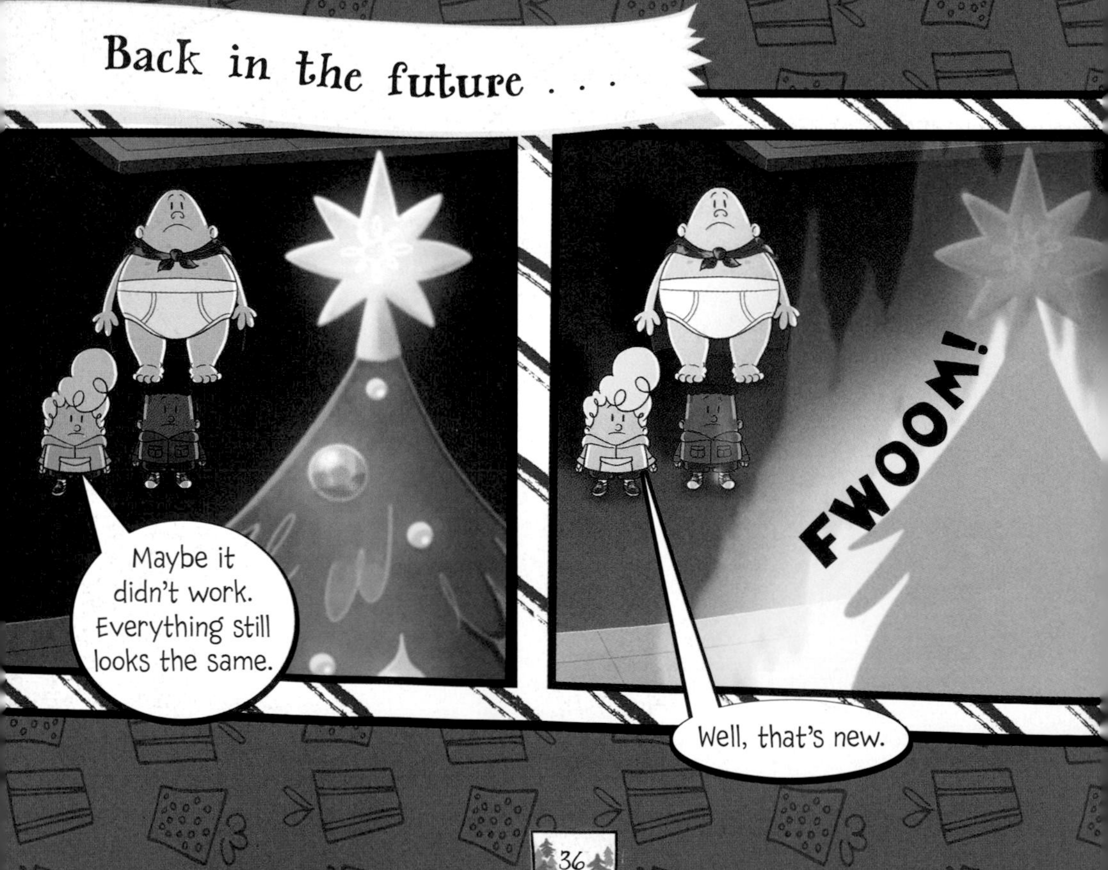
Back in the future . . .
Maybe it didn't work. Everything still looks the same.
FWOOM!
Well, that's new.

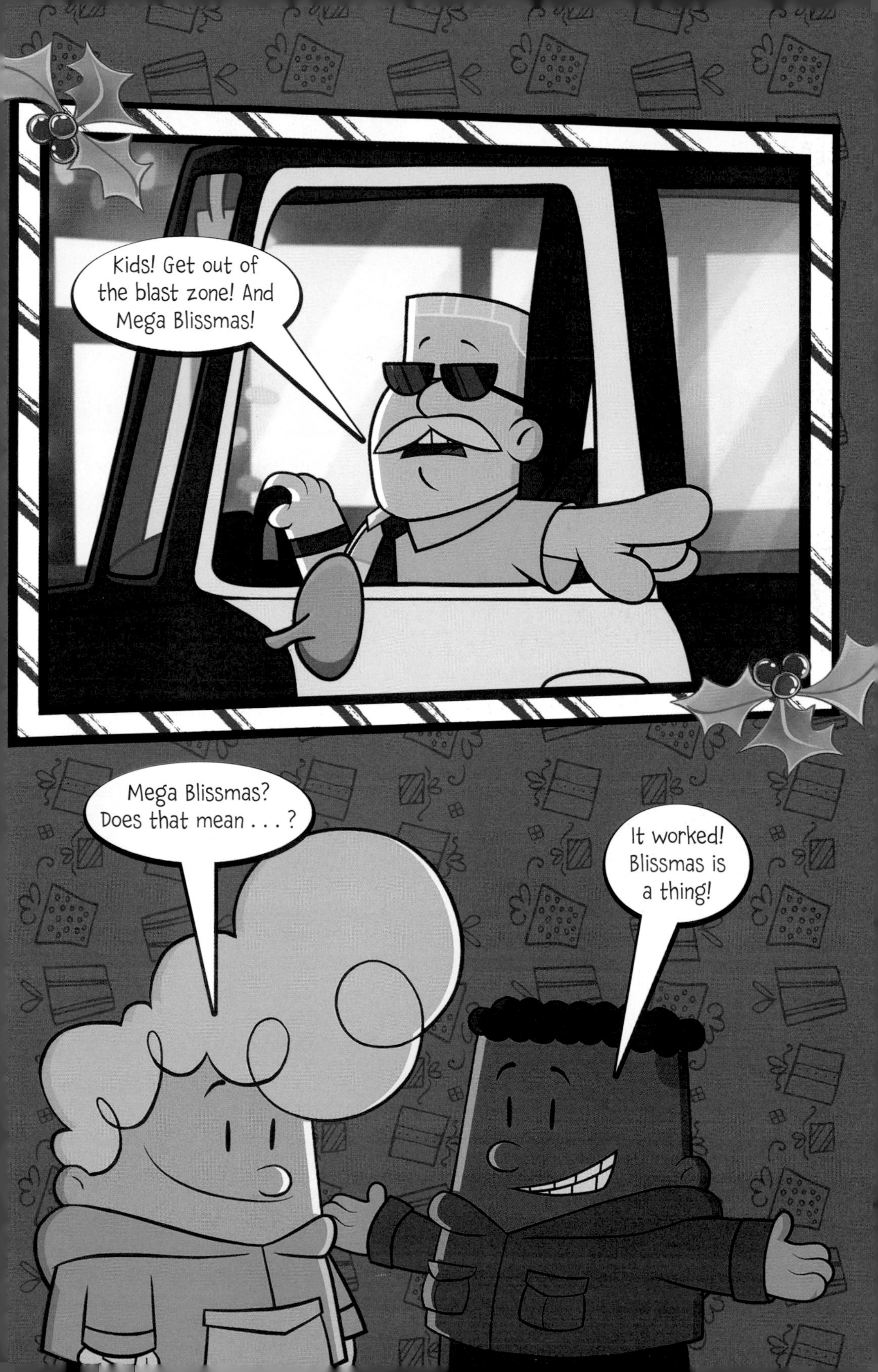
Kids! Get out of the blast zone! And Mega Blissmas!
Mega Blissmas? Does that mean . . . ?
It worked! Blissmas is a thing!

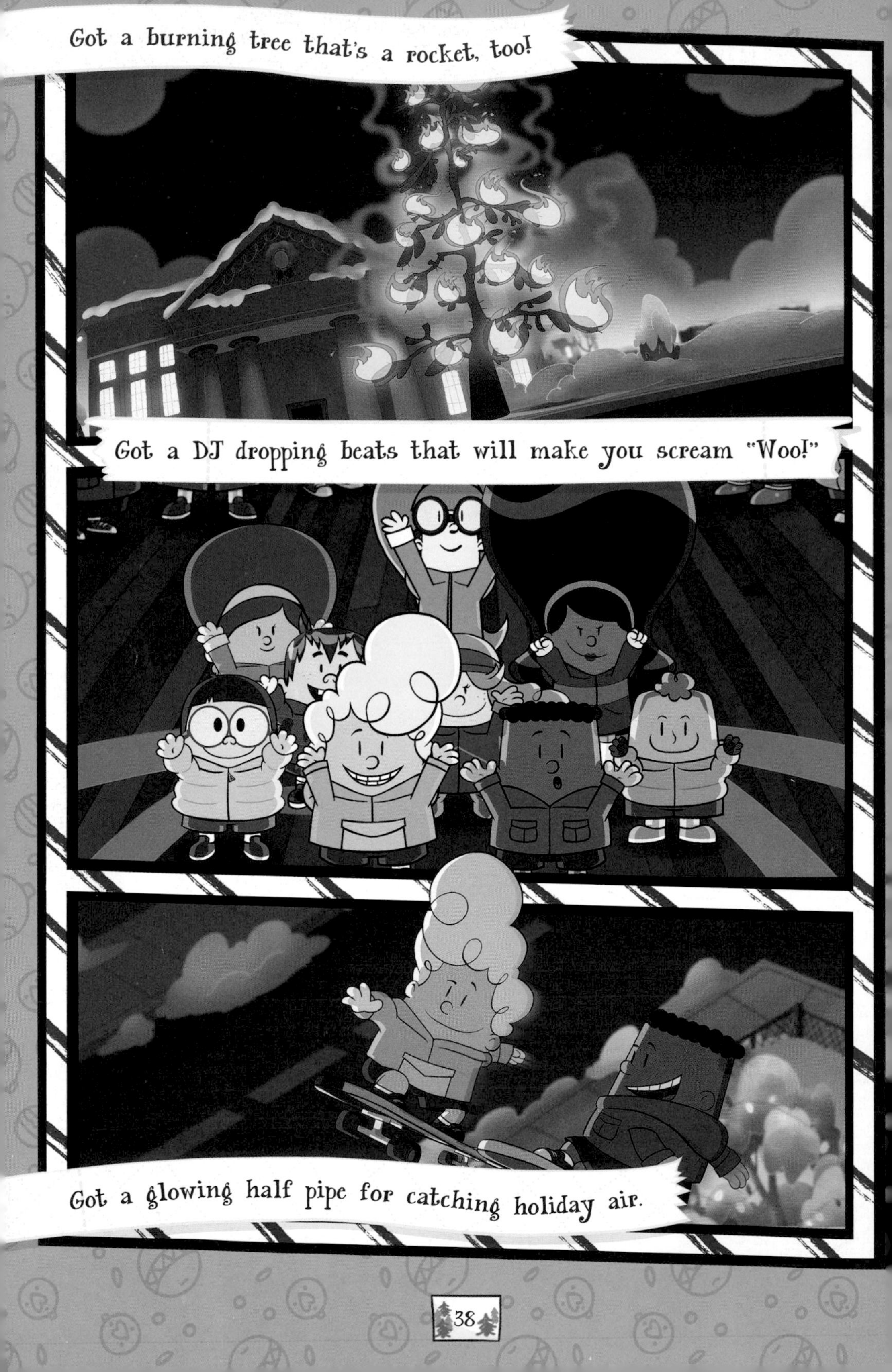
Got a burning tree that's a rocket, too!
Got a DJ dropping beats that will make you scream "Woo!"
Got a glowing half pipe for catching holiday air.

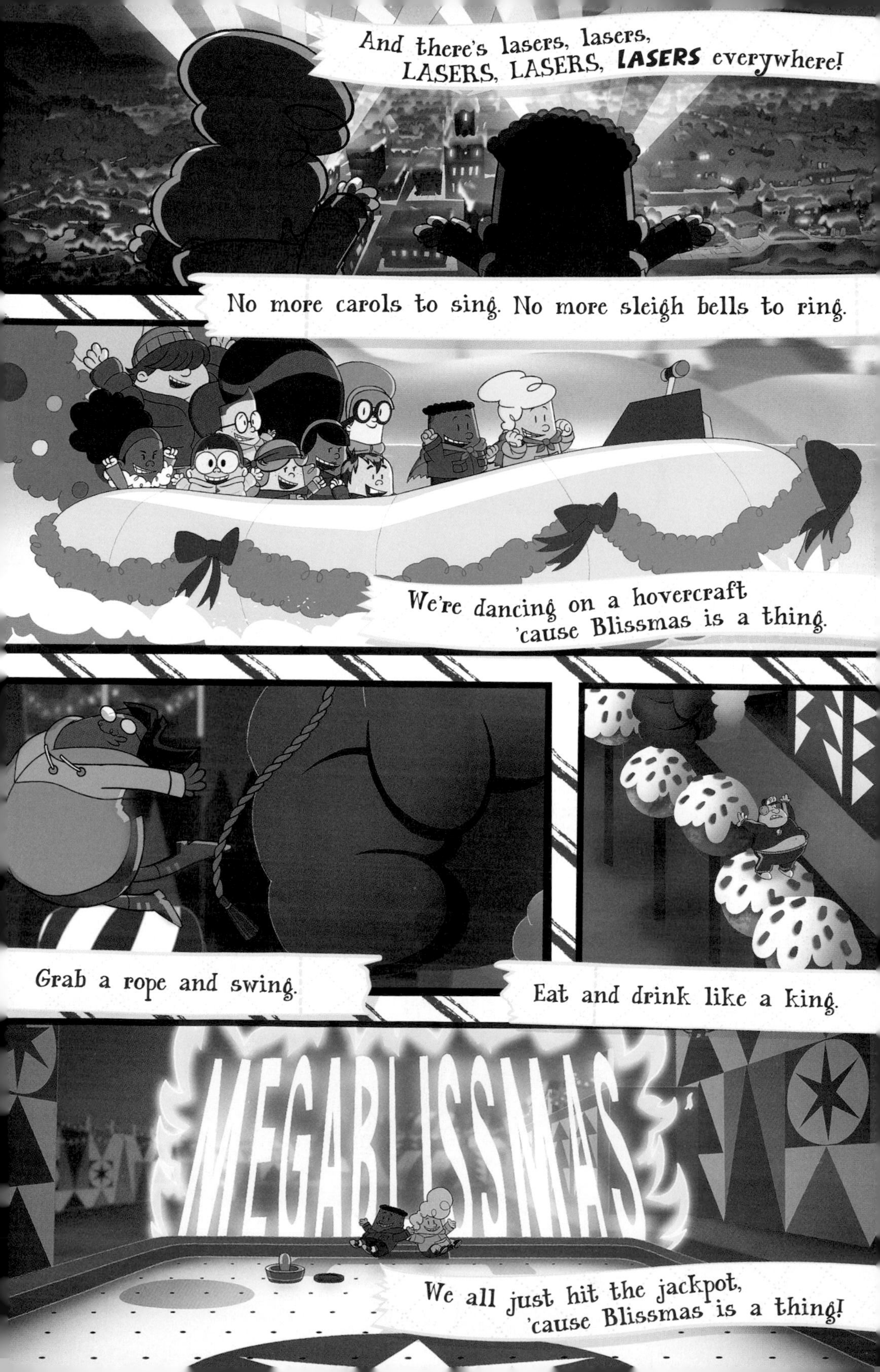
And there's lasers, lasers,
LASERS, LASERS, LASERS everywhere!
No more carols to sing. No more sleigh bells to ring.
We're dancing on a hovercraft
'cause Blissmas is a thing.
Grab a rope and swing.
Eat and drink like a king.
MEGABLISSMAS
We all just hit the jackpot,
'cause Blissmas is a thing!

While Captain Underpants flies off in search of some tra-la-treacle, George and Harold look for their friends to see if they're as excited about Blissmas as they are!

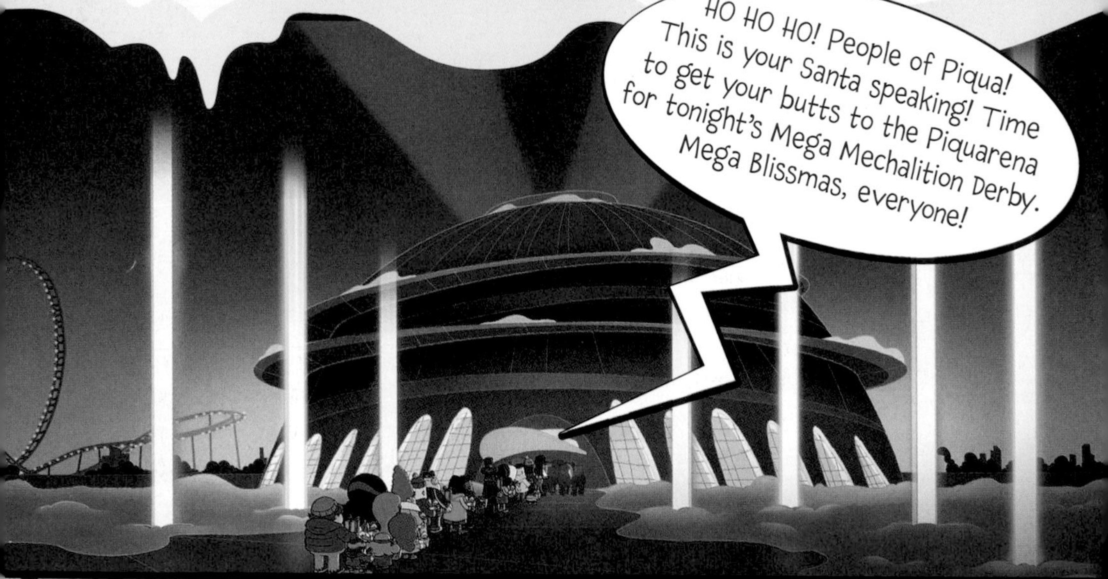
HO HO HO! People of Piqua! This is your Santa speaking! Time to get your butts to the Piquarena for tonight's Mega Mechalition Derby. Mega Blissmas, everyone!

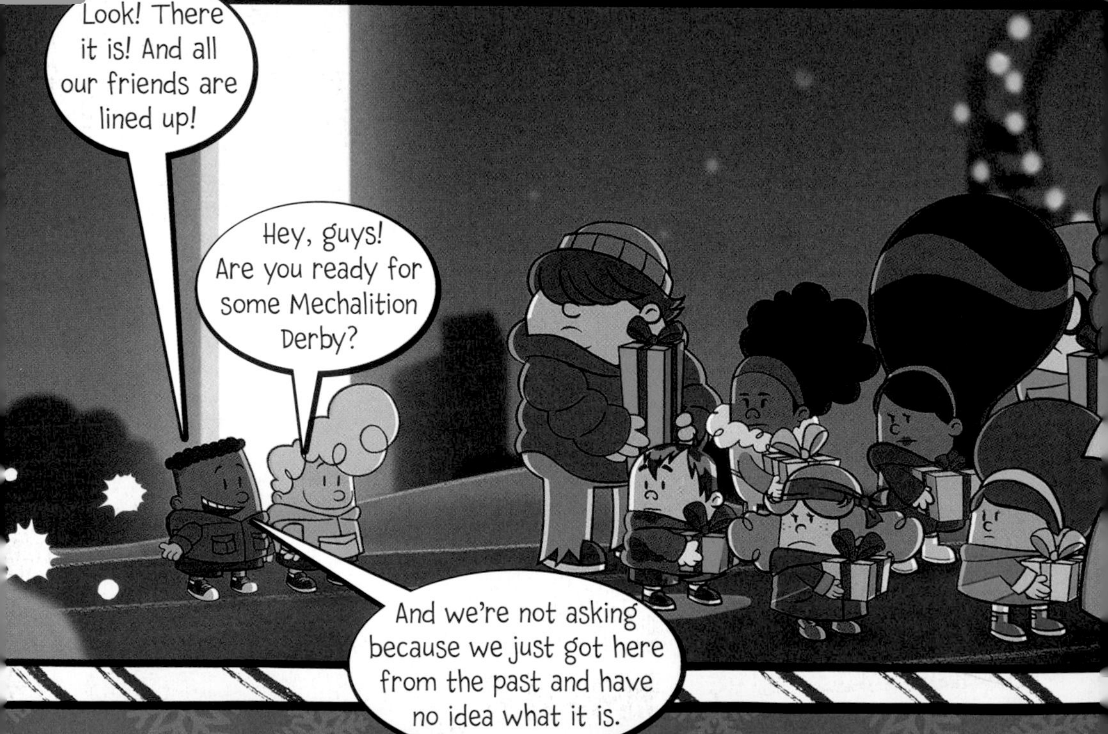
Look! There it is! And all our friends are lined up!
Hey, guys! Are you ready for some Mechalition Derby?
And we're not asking because we just got here from the past and have no idea what it is.

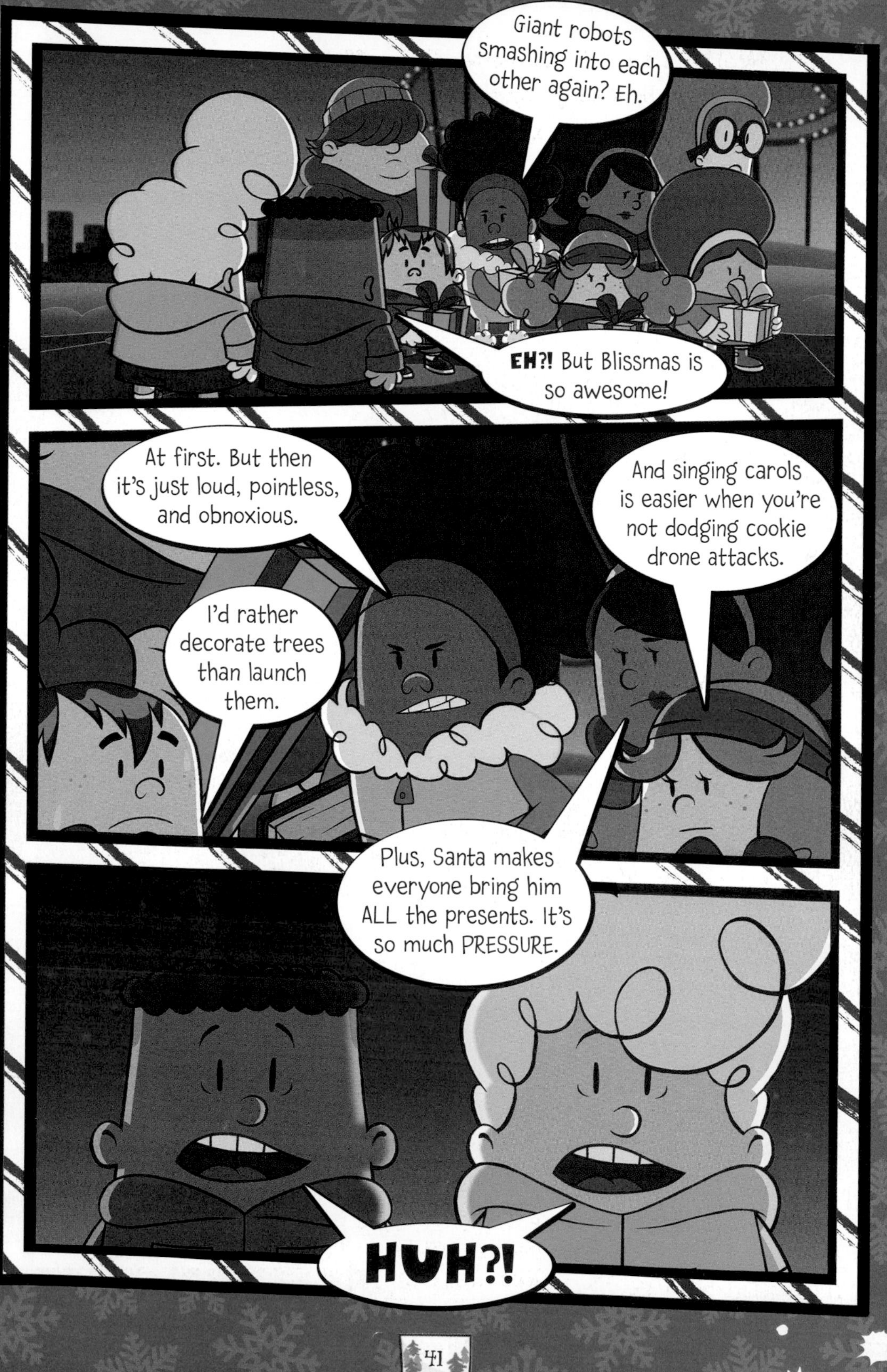
Giant robots smashing into each other again? Eh.
EH?! But Blissmas is so awesome!
At first. But then it's just loud, pointless, and obnoxious.
And singing carols is easier when you're not dodging cookie drone attacks.
I'd rather decorate trees than launch them.
Plus, Santa makes everyone bring him ALL the presents. It's so much PRESSURE.
HUH?!

CHAPTER 8

SANTA FLAWS

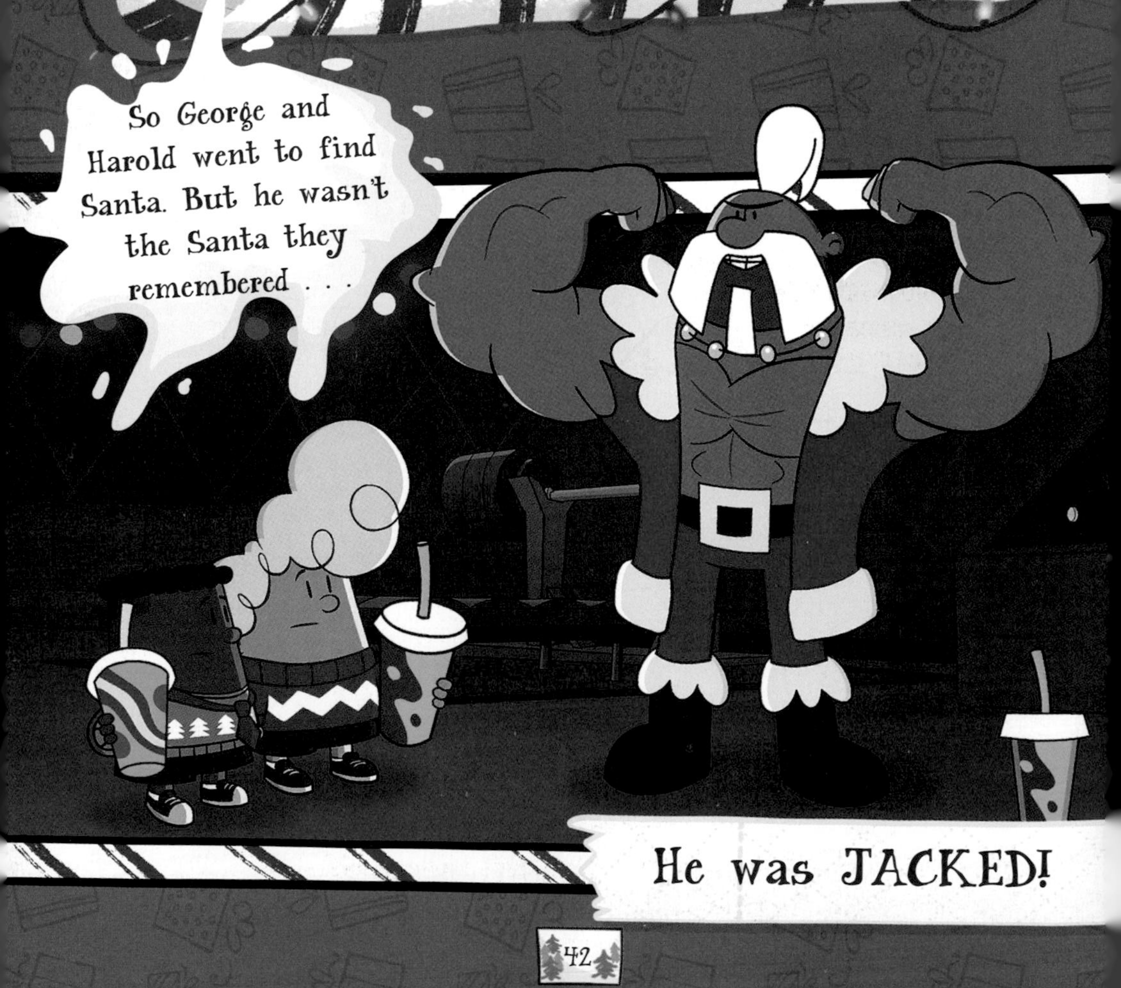
So George and Harold went to find Santa. But he wasn't the Santa they remembered . . .
He was JACKED!

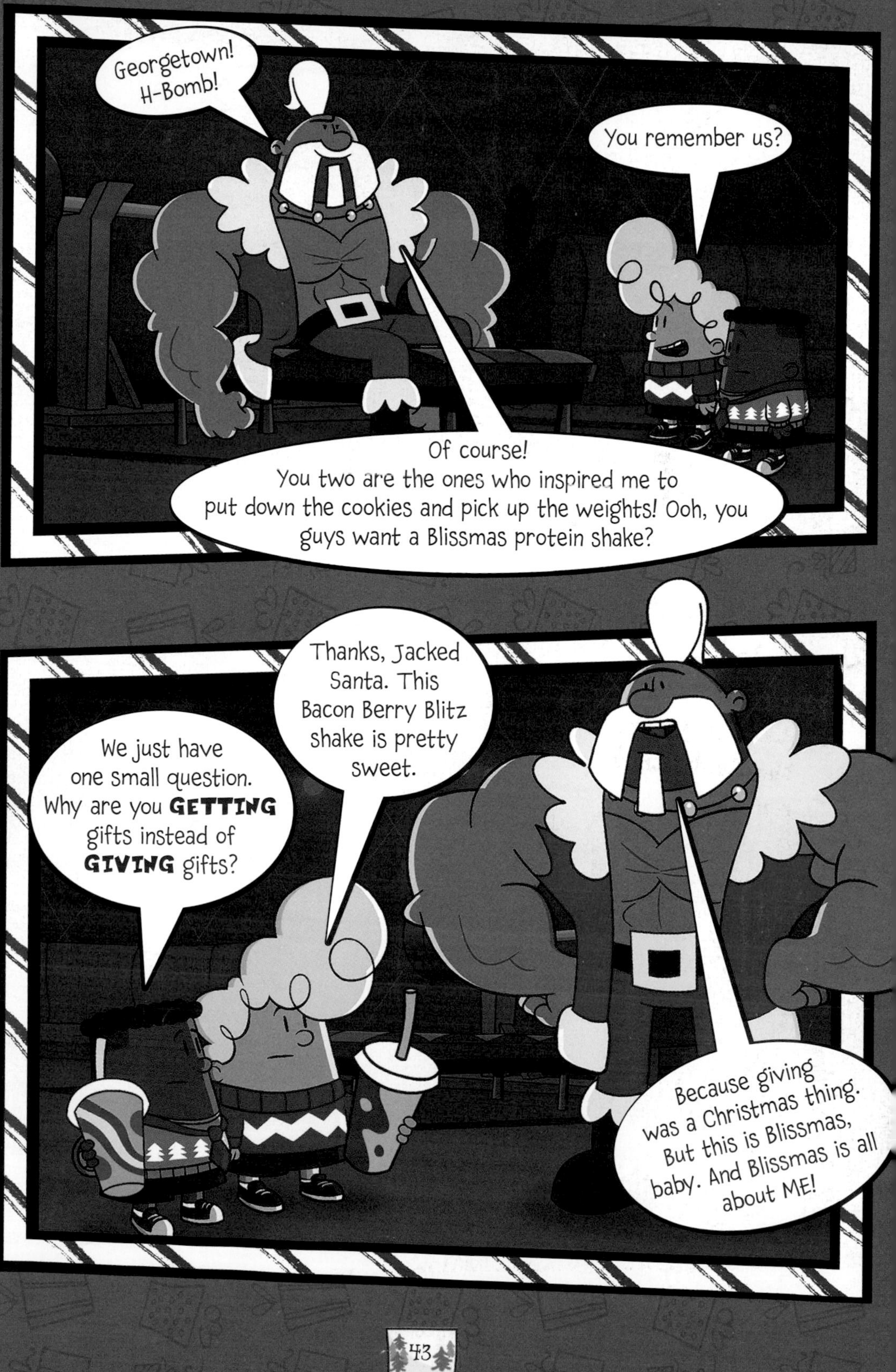
Georgetown! H-Bomb!
You remember us?
Of course! You two are the ones who inspired me to put down the cookies and pick up the weights! Ooh, you guys want a Blissmas protein shake?
Thanks, Jacked Santa. This Bacon Berry Blitz shake is pretty sweet.
We just have one small question. Why are you GETTING gifts instead of GIVING gifts?
Because giving was a Christmas thing. But this is Blissmas, baby. And Blissmas is all about ME!

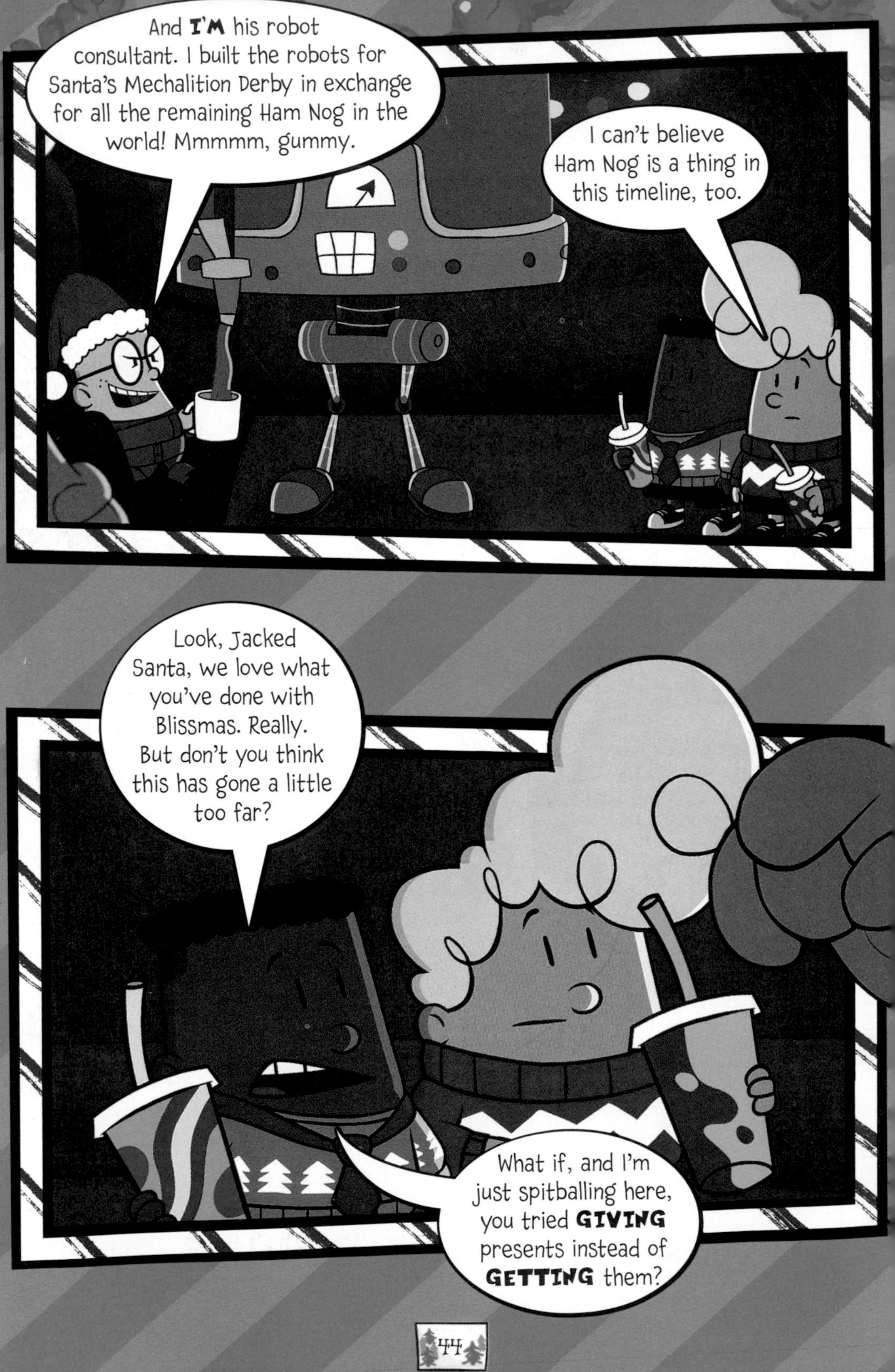
And I'M his robot consultant. I built the robots for Santa's Mechalition Derby in exchange for all the remaining Ham Nog in the world! Mmmmm, gummy.
I can't believe Ham Nog is a thing in this timeline, too.
Look, Jacked Santa, we love what you've done with Blissmas. Really. But don't you think this has gone a little too far?
What if, and I'm just spitballing here, you tried GIVING presents instead of GETTING them?

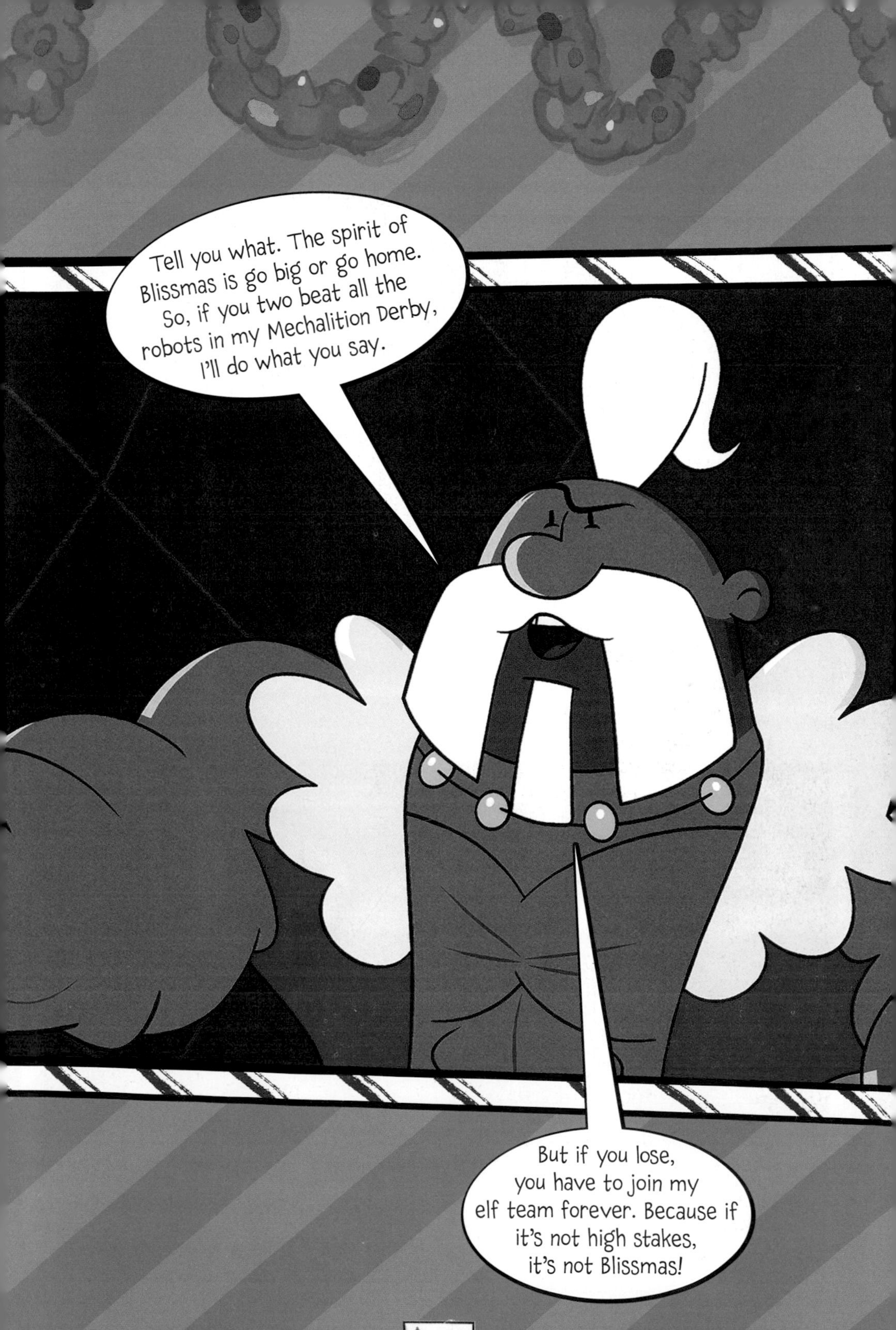
Tell you what. The spirit of Blissmas is go big or go home. So, if you two beat all the robots in my Mechalition Derby, I'll do what you say.
But if you lose, you have to join my elf team forever. Because if it's not high stakes, it's not Blissmas!

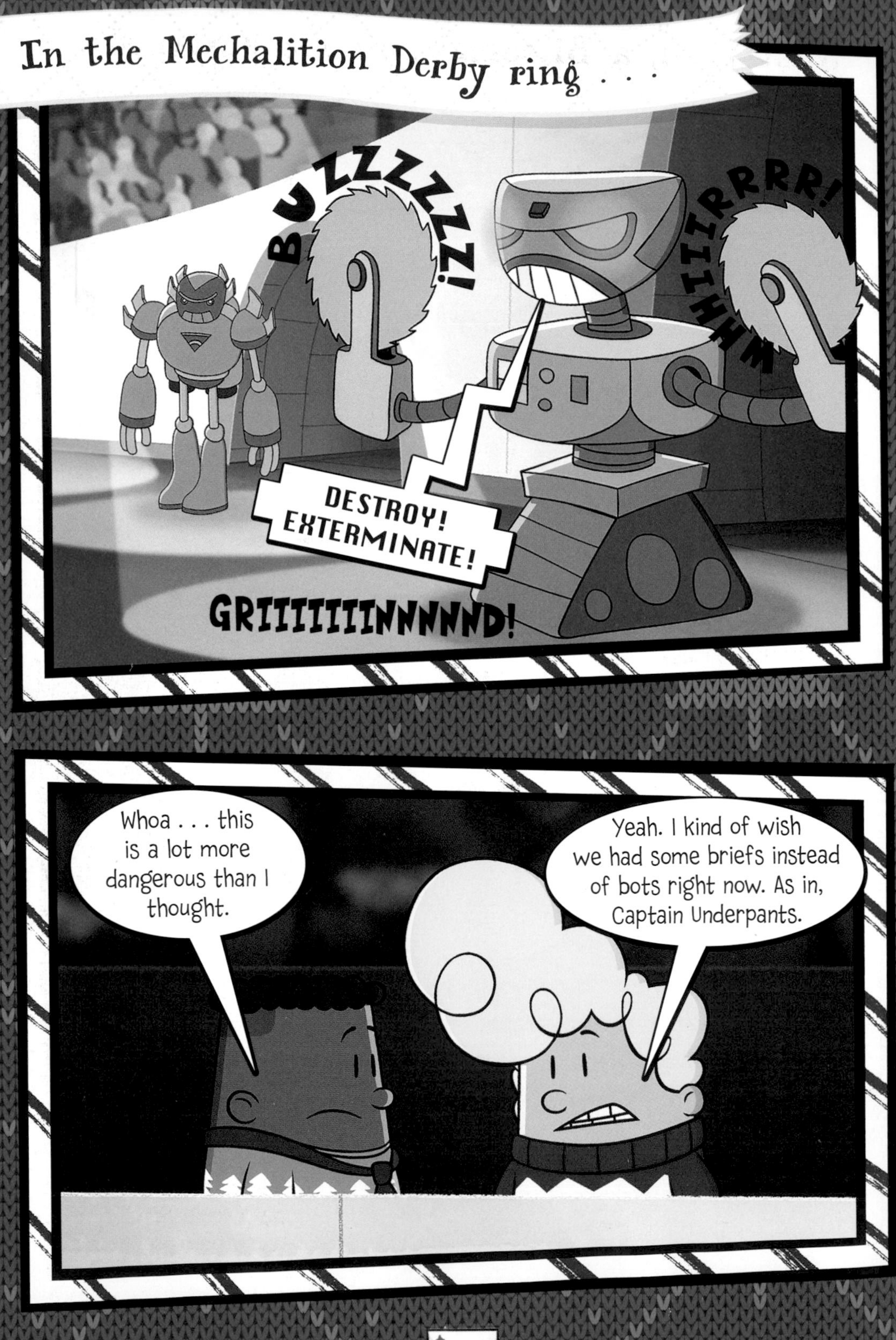
In the Mechalition Derby ring . . .
BUZZZZZZZ!
WHHHIIIIRRRRR!
DESTROY! EXTERMINATE!
GRIIIIIIINNNNND!
Whoa . . . this is a lot more dangerous than I thought.
Yeah. I kind of wish we had some briefs instead of bots right now. As in, Captain Underpants.

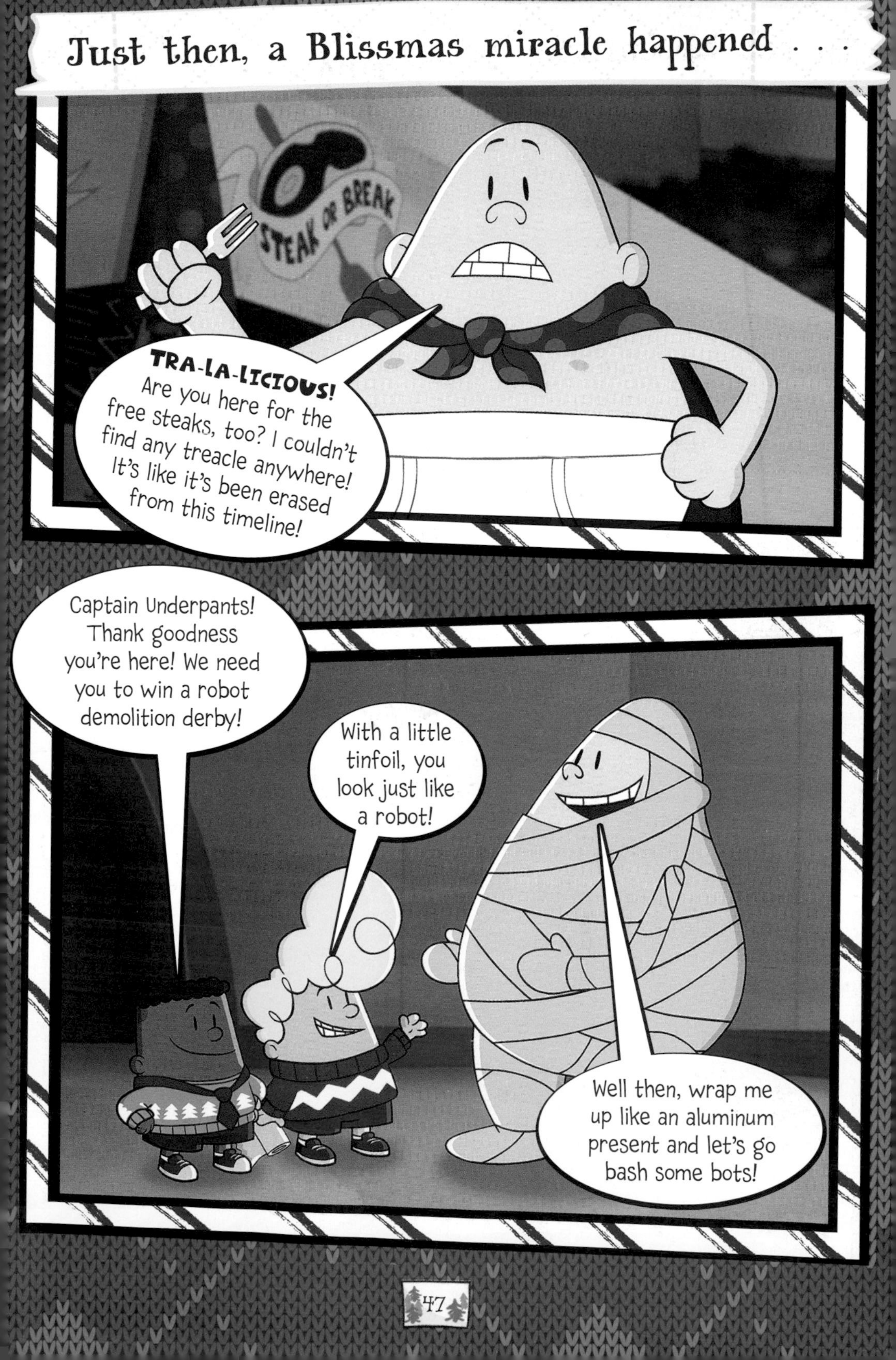
Just then, a Blissmas miracle happened . . .
STEAK OR BREAK
TRA-LA-LICIOUS! Are you here for the free steaks, too? I couldn't find any treacle anywhere! It's like it's been erased from this timeline!
Captain Underpants! Thank goodness you're here! We need you to win a robot demolition derby!
With a little tinfoil, you look just like a robot!
Well then, wrap me up like an aluminum present and let's go bash some bots!

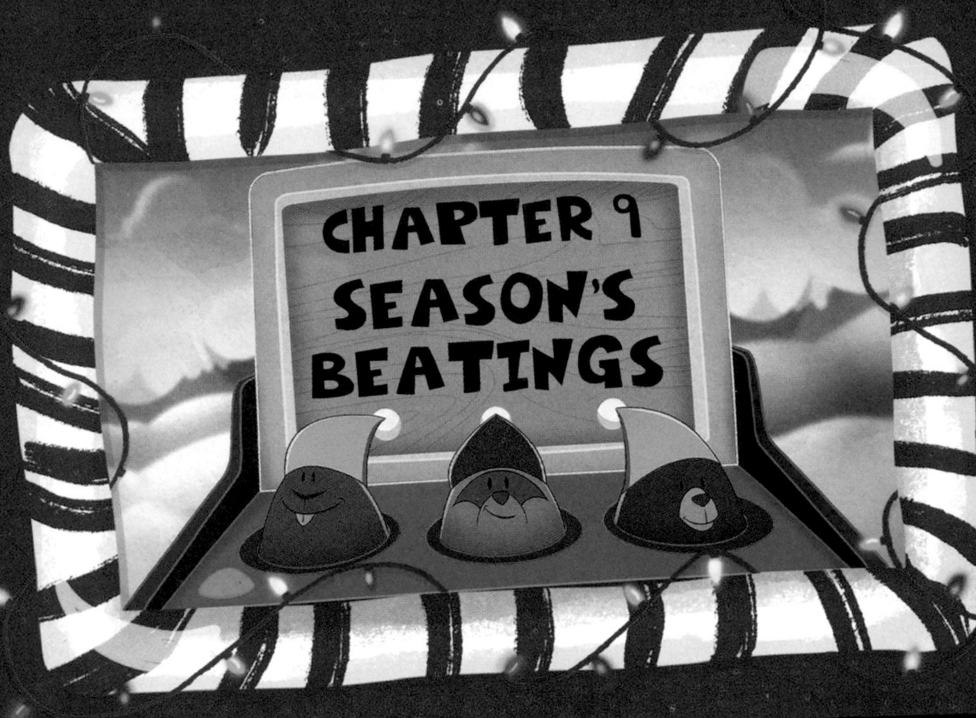

CHAPTER 9
SEASON'S BEATINGS

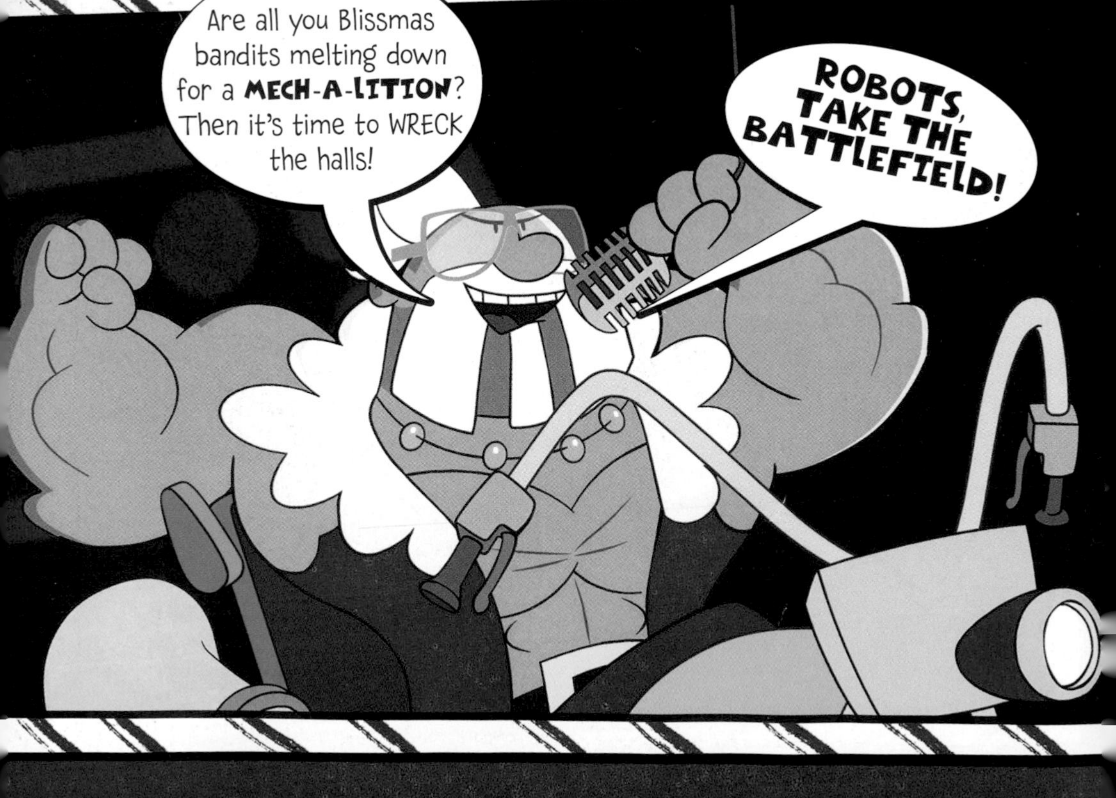

Are all you Blissmas bandits melting down for a MECH-A-LITION? Then it's time to WRECK the halls!
ROBOTS, TAKE THE BATTLEFIELD!

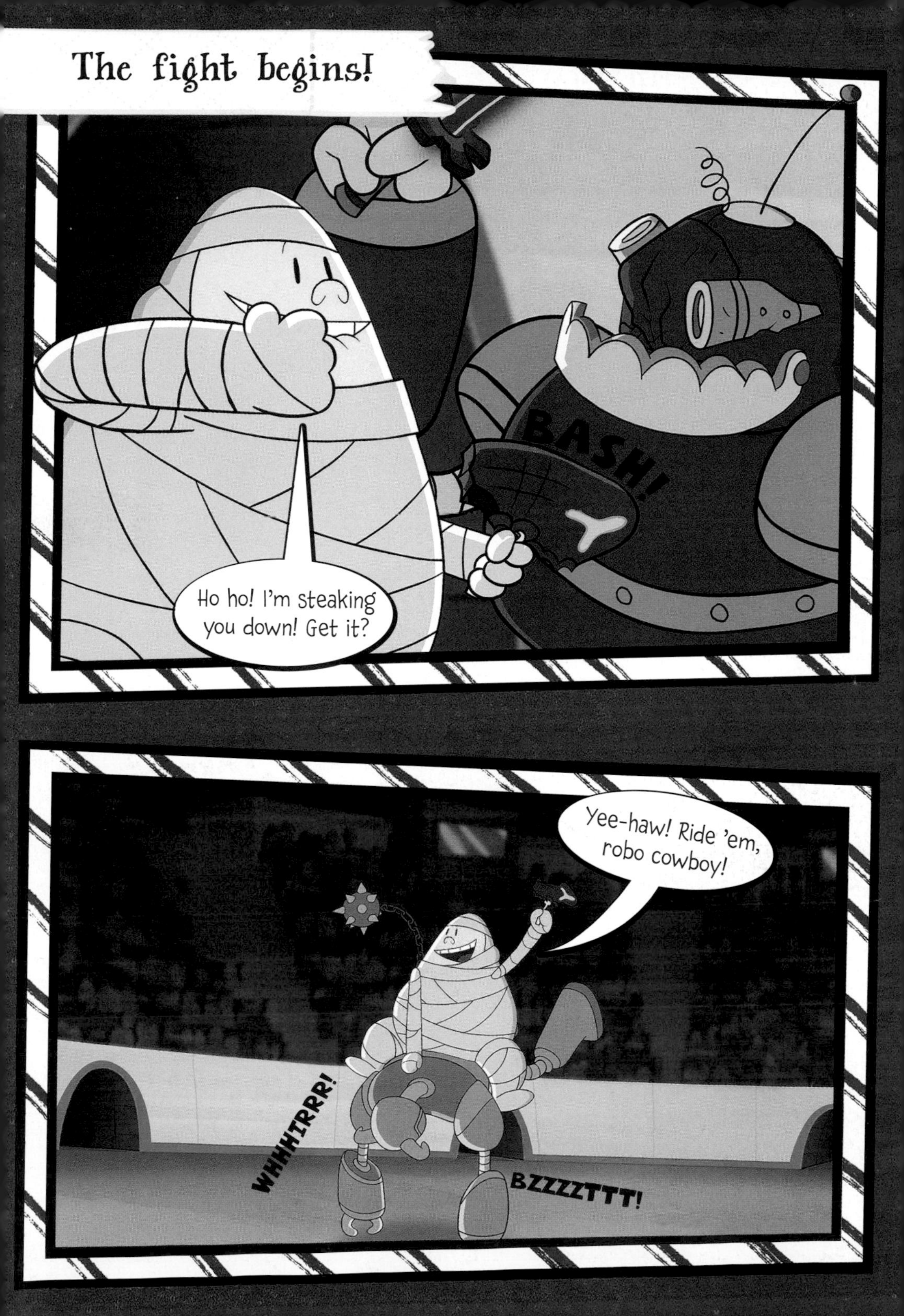
The fight begins!
BASH!
Ho ho! I'm steaking you down! Get it?
Yee-haw! Ride 'em, robo cowboy!
WHHHIRRR!
BZZZZTTT!

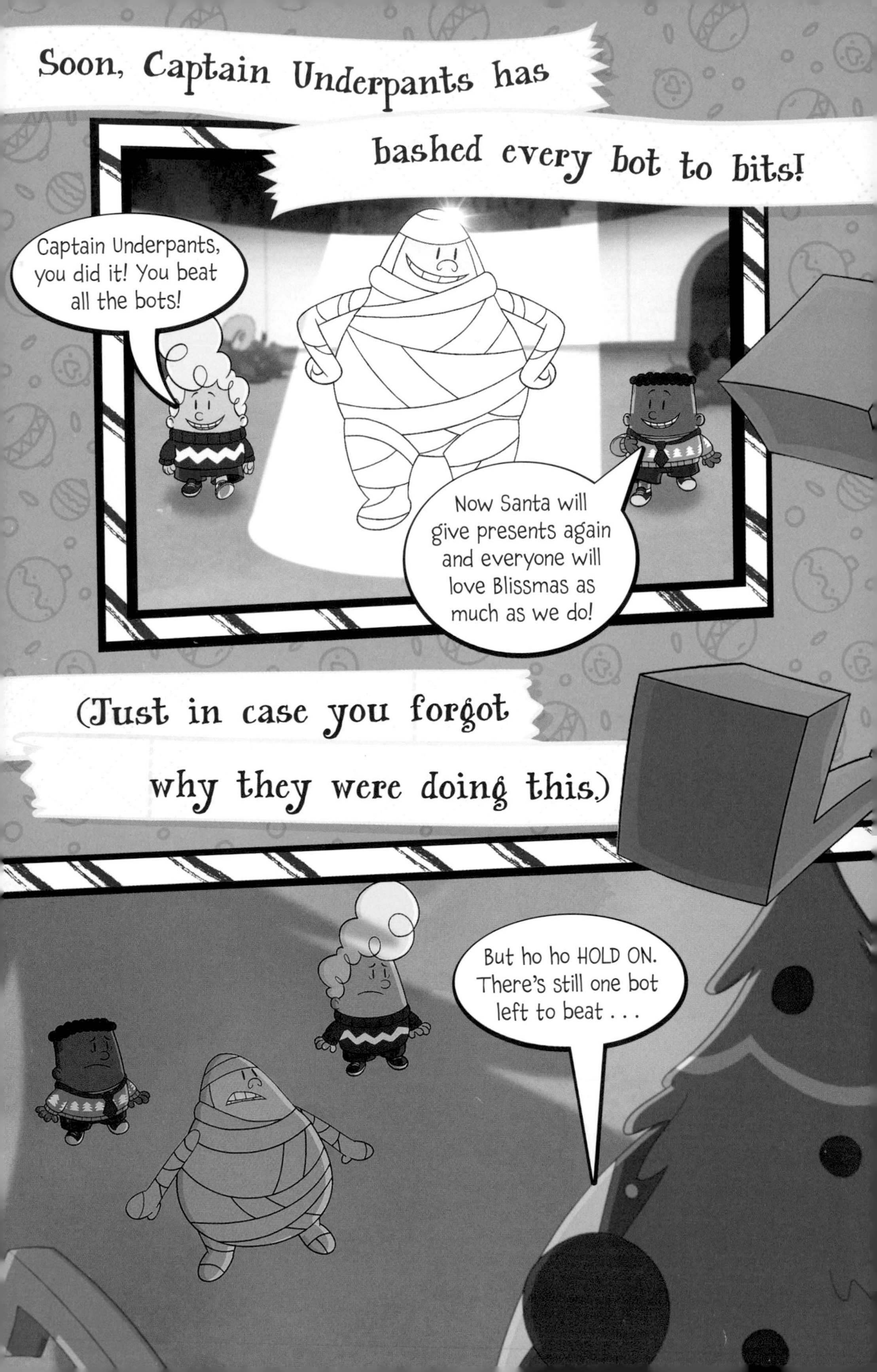
Soon, Captain Underpants has
bashed every bot to bits!
Captain Underpants, you did it! You beat all the bots!
Now Santa will give presents again and everyone will love Blissmas as much as we do!
(Just in case you forgot why they were doing this.)
But ho ho HOLD ON. There's still one bot left to beat . . .

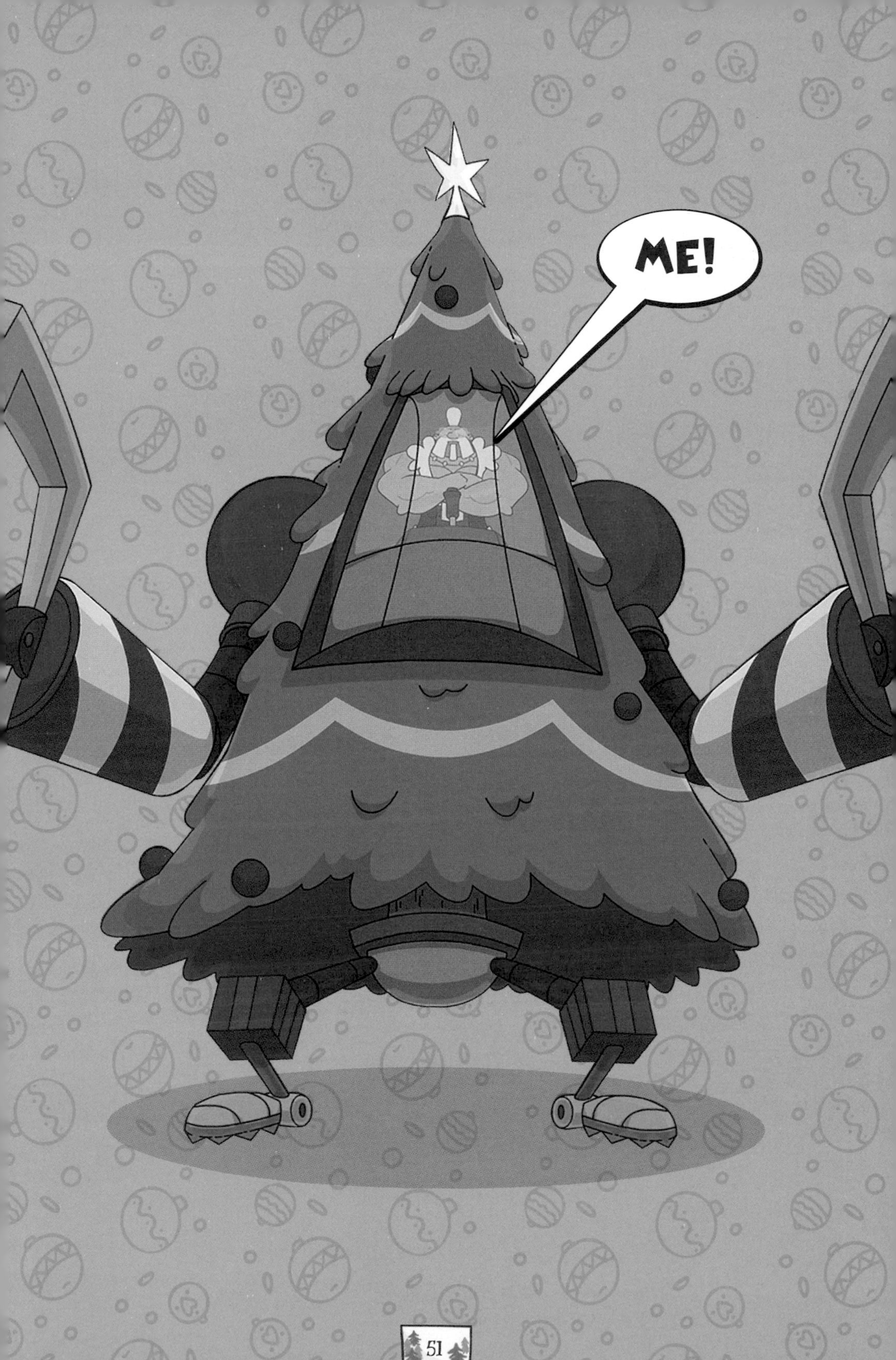
ME!

CHAPTER 10
THE INCREDIBLY GRAPHIC VIOLENCE CHAPTER

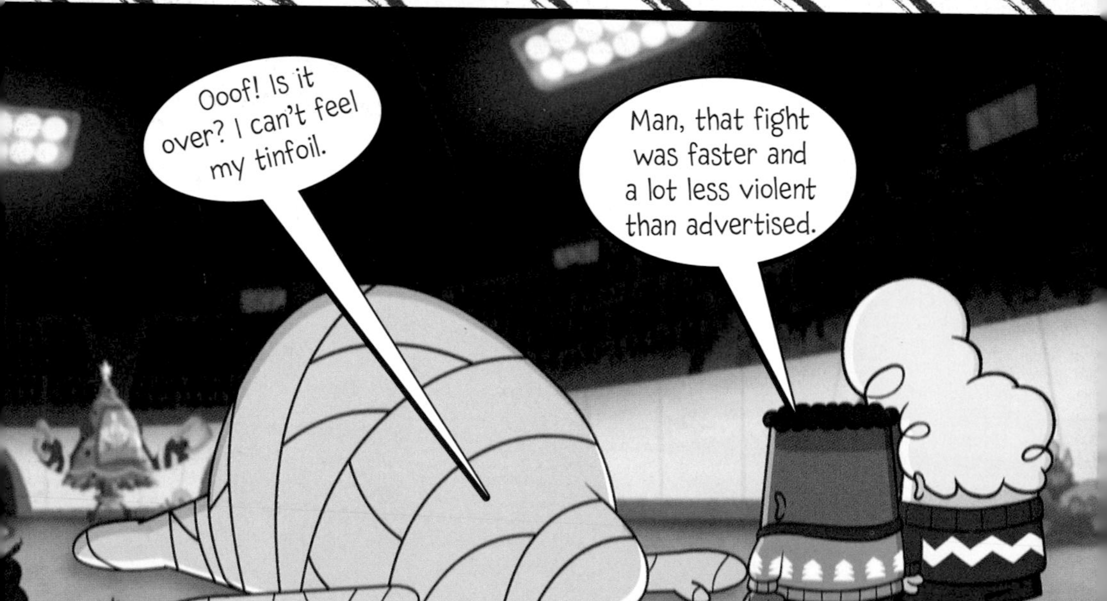

Ooof! Is it over? I can't feel my tinfoil.
Man, that fight was faster and a lot less violent than advertised.

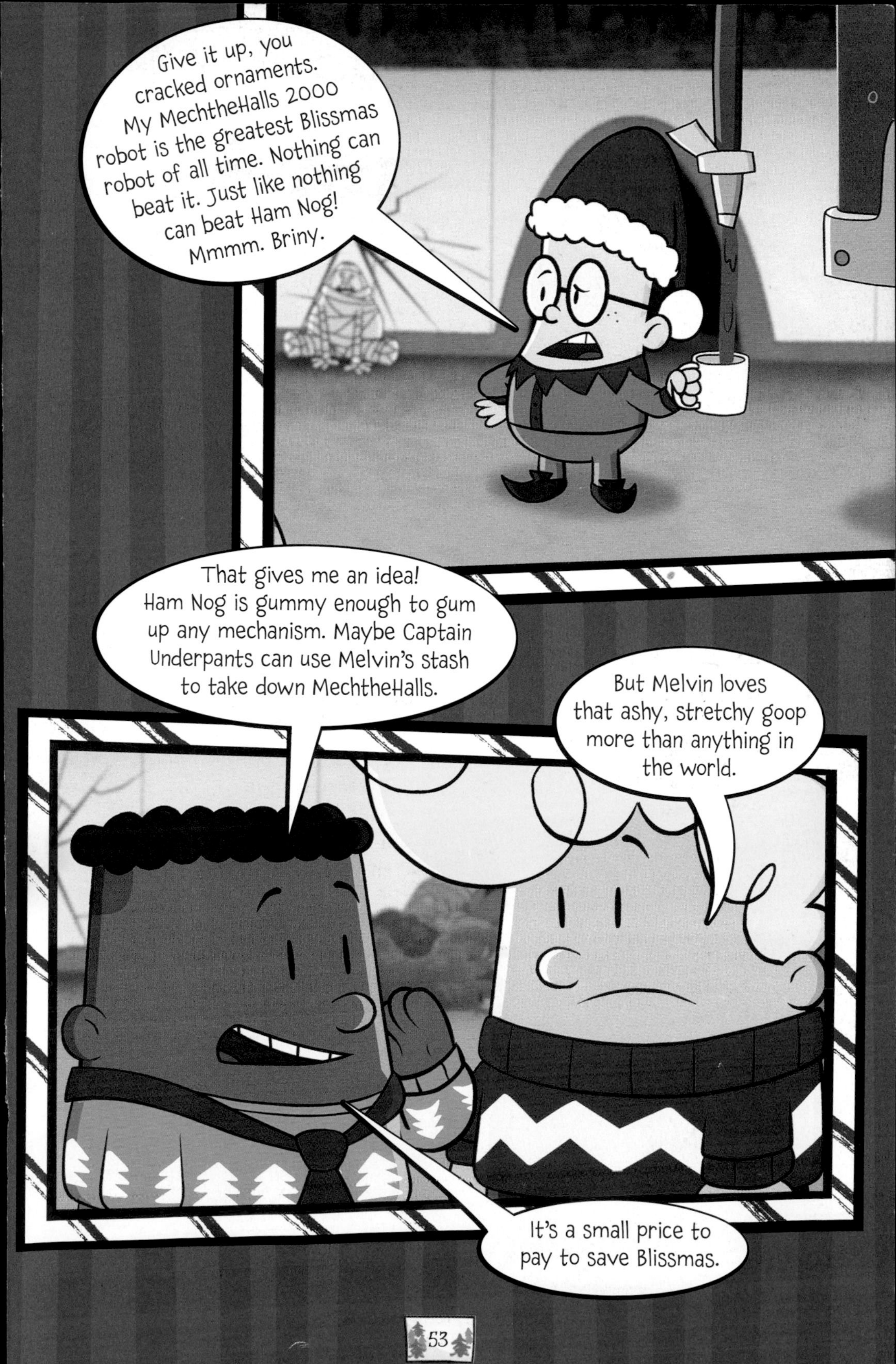
Give it up, you cracked ornaments. My MechtheHalls 2000 robot is the greatest Blissmas robot of all time. Nothing can beat it. Just like nothing can beat Ham Nog! Mmmm. Briny.
That gives me an idea! Ham Nog is gummy enough to gum up any mechanism. Maybe Captain Underpants can use Melvin's stash to take down MechtheHalls.
But Melvin loves that ashy, stretchy goop more than anything in the world.
It's a small price to pay to save Blissmas.

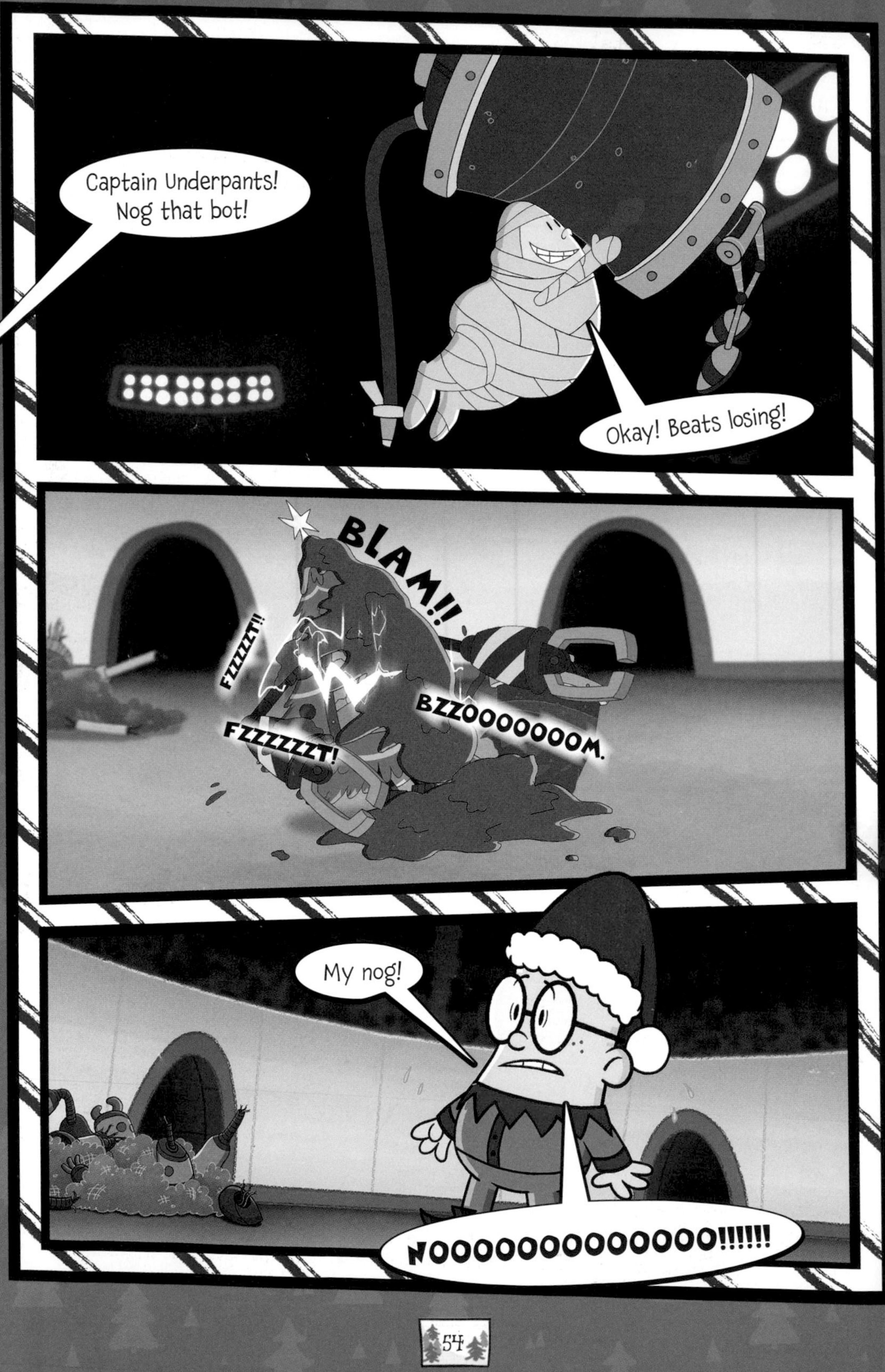
Captain Underpants! Nog that bot!
Okay! Beats losing!
BLAM!!
FZZZZZT!!
BZZOOOOOOOOM.
FZZZZZZZT!
My nog!
NOOOOOOOOOOOOOO!!!!!!

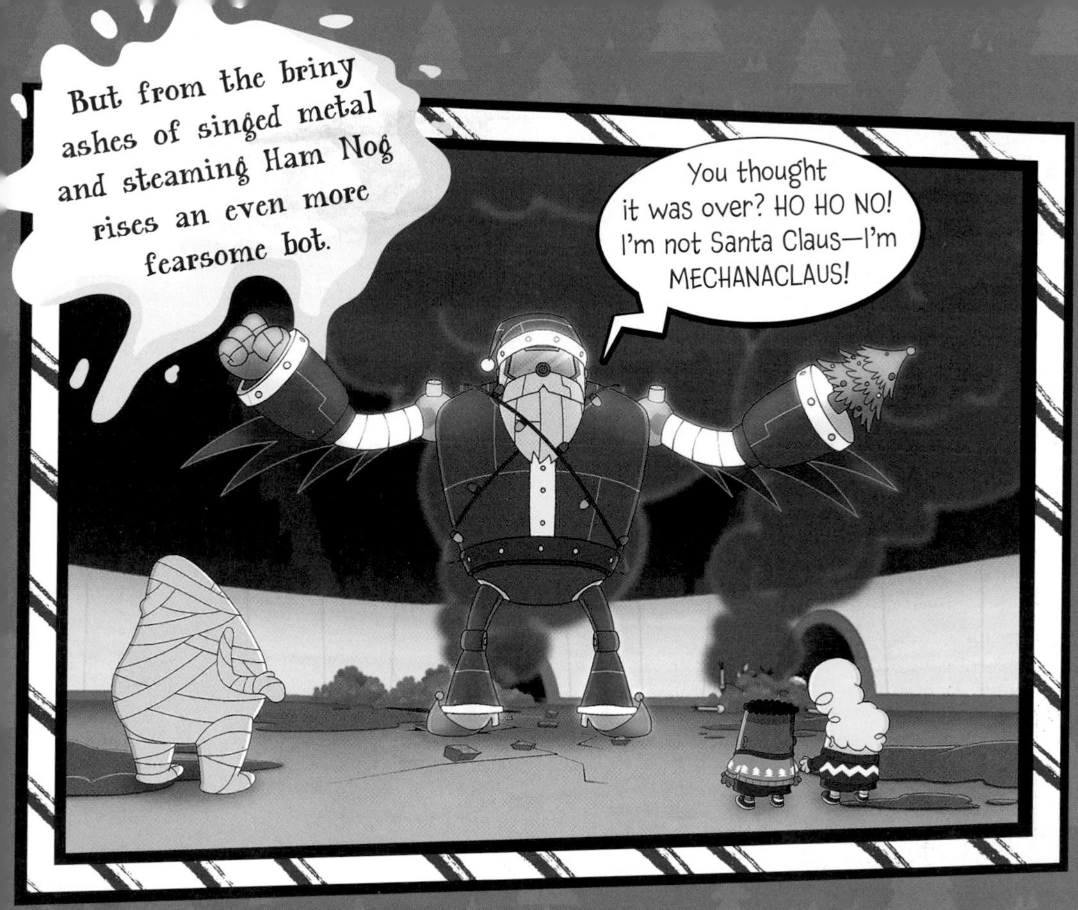
But from the briny ashes of singed metal and steaming Ham Nog rises an even more fearsome bot.
You thought it was over? HO HO NO! I'm not Santa Claus—I'm MECHANACLAUS!

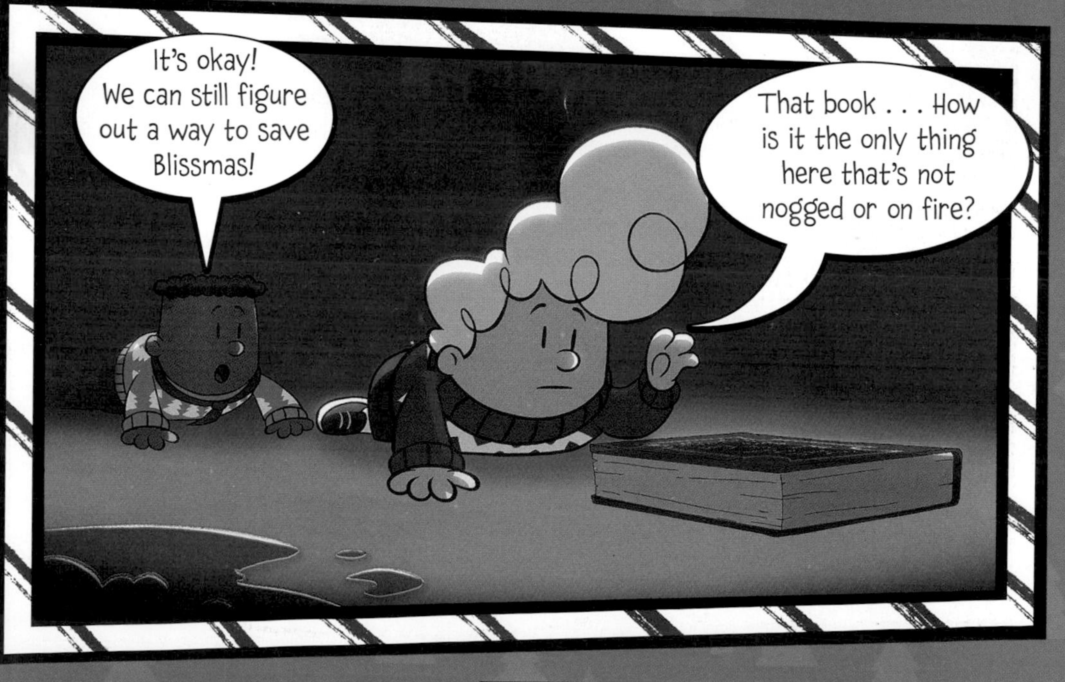
It's okay! We can still figure out a way to save Blissmas!
That book . . . How is it the only thing here that's not nogged or on fire?

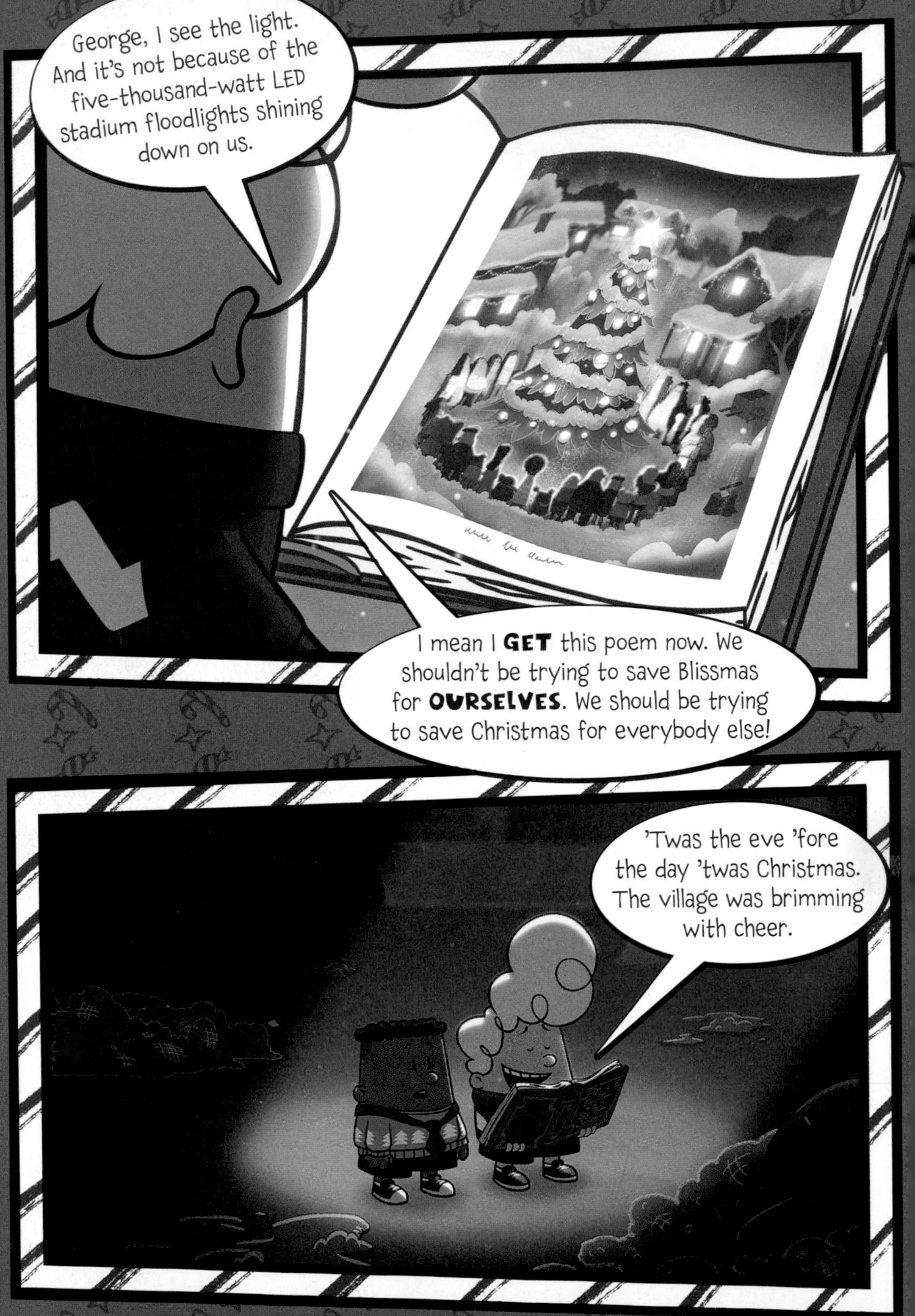
George, I see the light. And it's not because of the five-thousand-watt LED stadium floodlights shining down on us.
I mean I **GET** this poem now. We shouldn't be trying to save Blissmas for **OURSELVES**. We should be trying to save Christmas for everybody else!
'Twas the eve 'fore the day 'twas Christmas. The village was brimming with cheer.

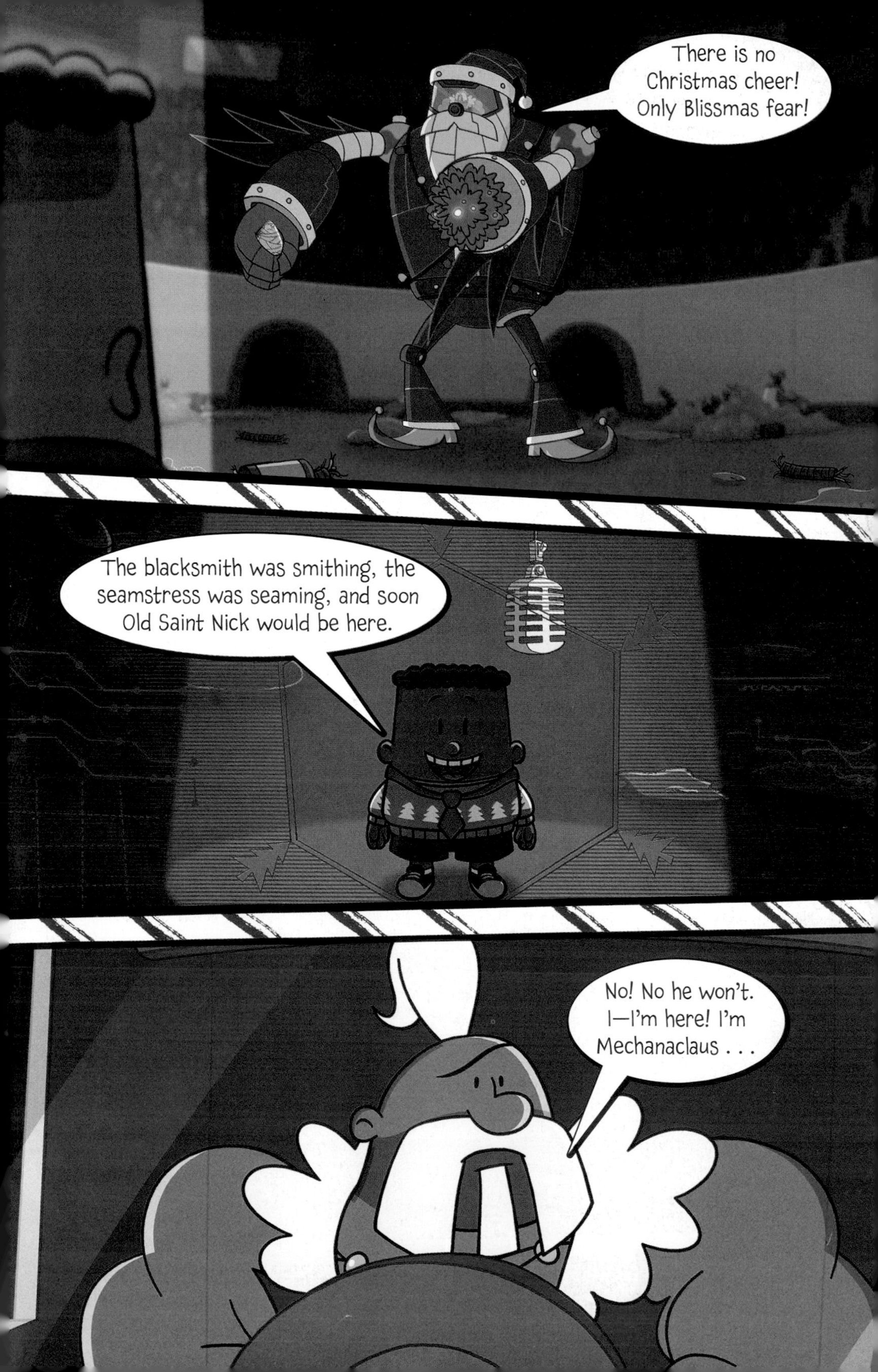
There is no Christmas cheer! Only Blissmas fear!
The blacksmith was smithing, the seamstress was seaming, and soon Old Saint Nick would be here.
No! No he won't. I—I'm here! I'm Mechanaclaus . . .

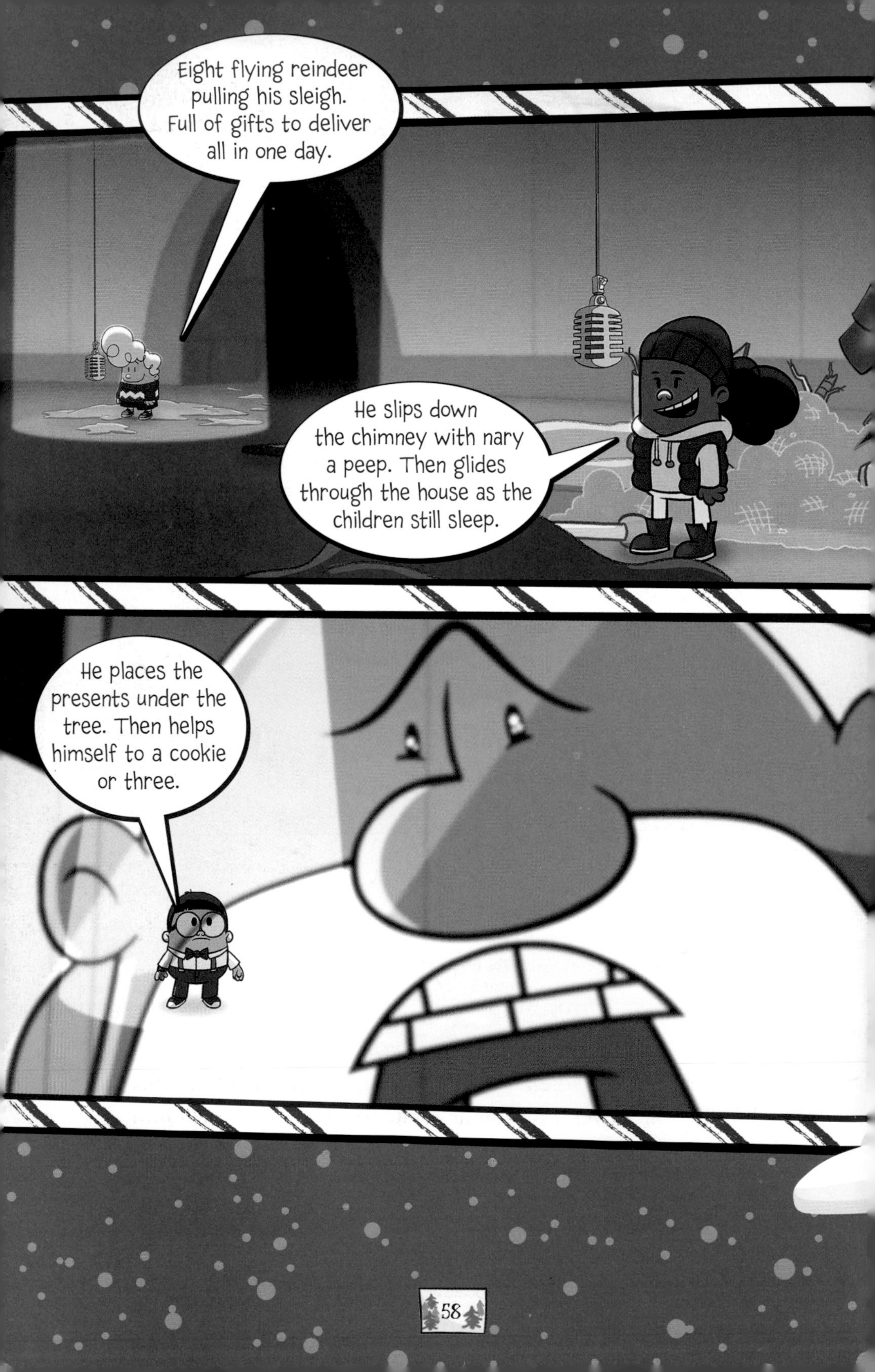
Eight flying reindeer pulling his sleigh. Full of gifts to deliver all in one day.
He slips down the chimney with nary a peep. Then glides through the house as the children still sleep.
He places the presents under the tree. Then helps himself to a cookie or three.

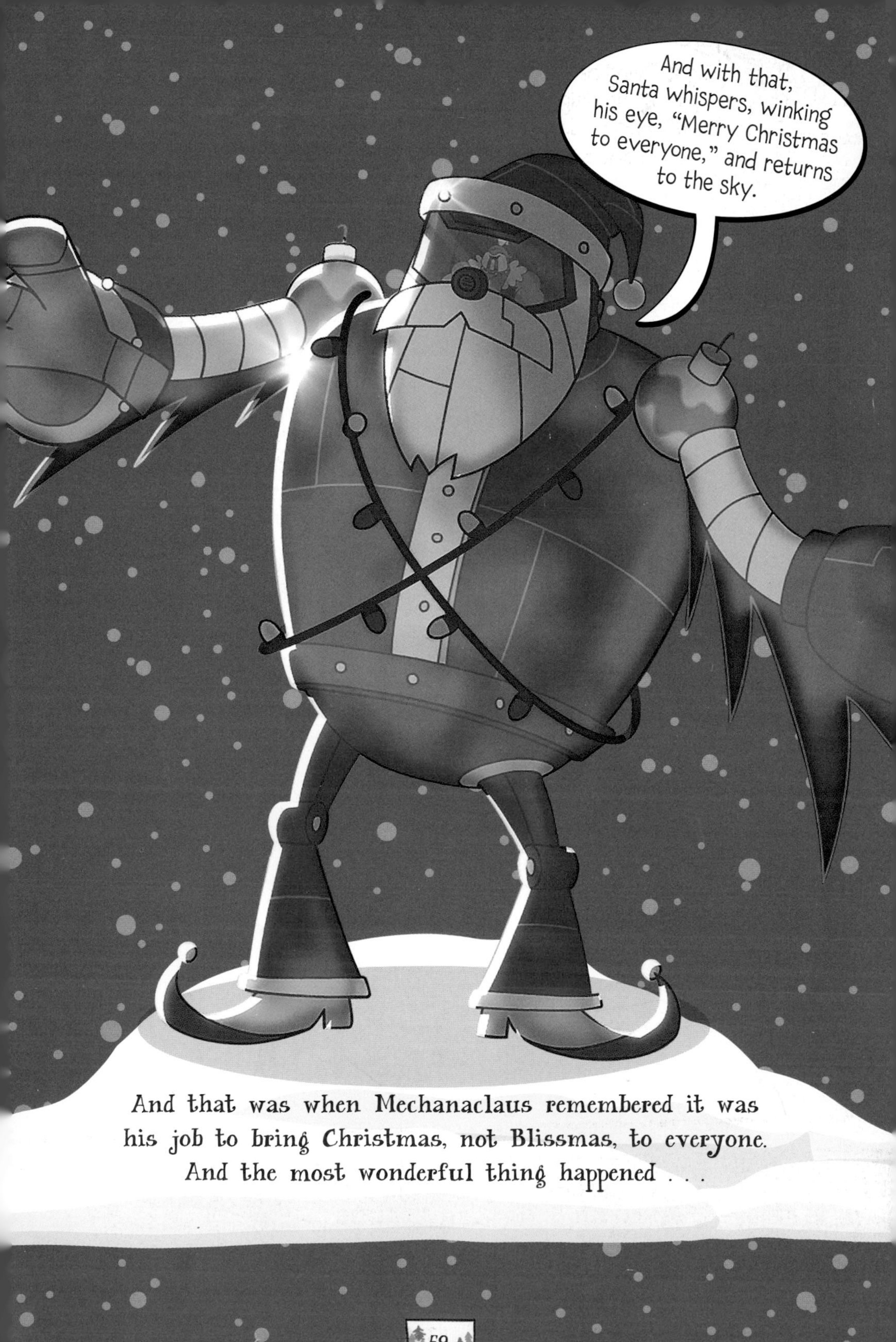
And with that, Santa whispers, winking his eye, "Merry Christmas to everyone," and returns to the sky.

And that was when Mechanaclaus remembered it was his job to bring Christmas, not Blissmas, to everyone. And the most wonderful thing happened . . .

Mechanaclaus became the Santa Claus he was supposed to be!

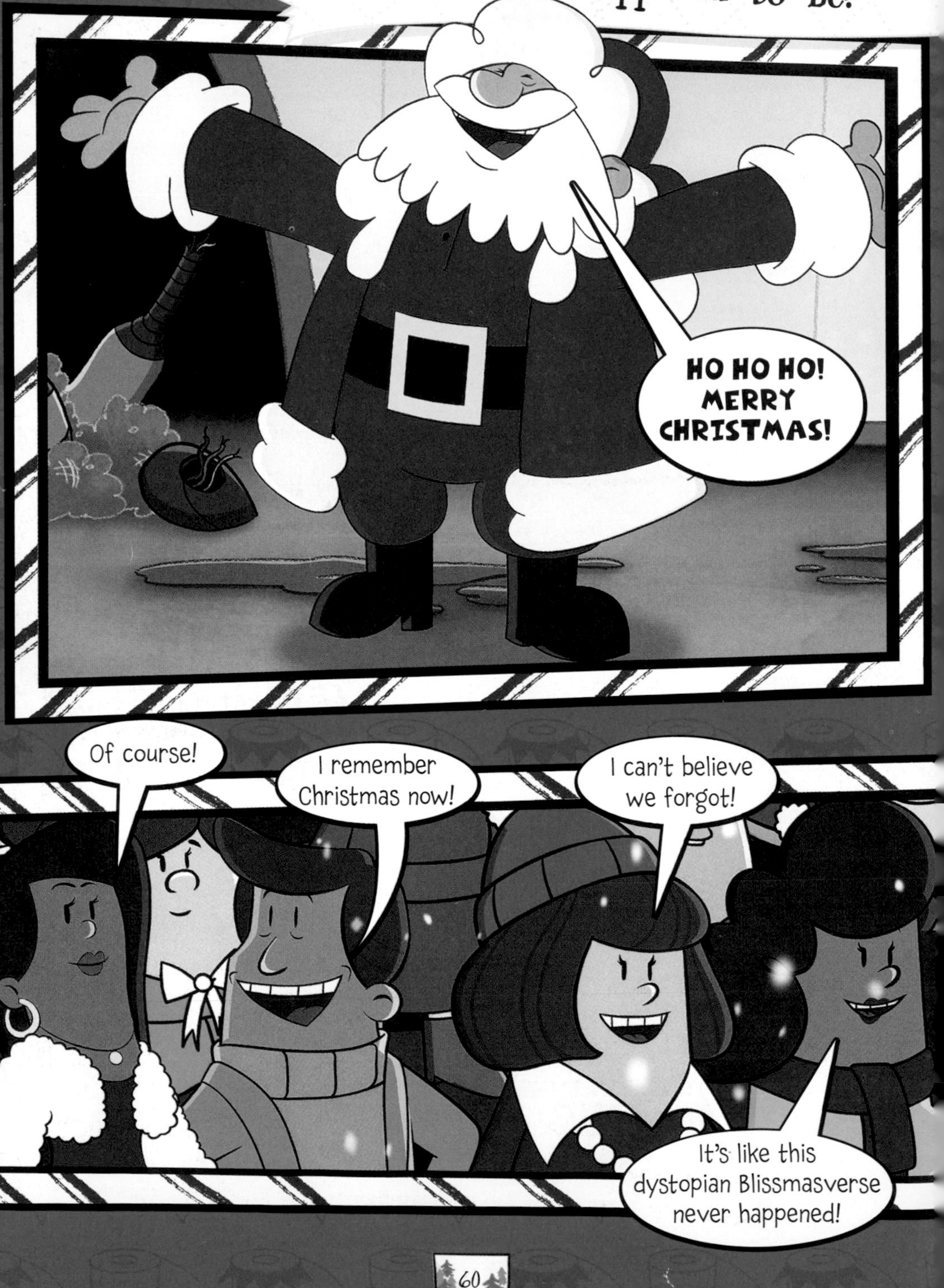
HO HO HO! MERRY CHRISTMAS!
Of course!
I remember Christmas now!
I can't believe we forgot!
It's like this dystopian Blissmasverse never happened!

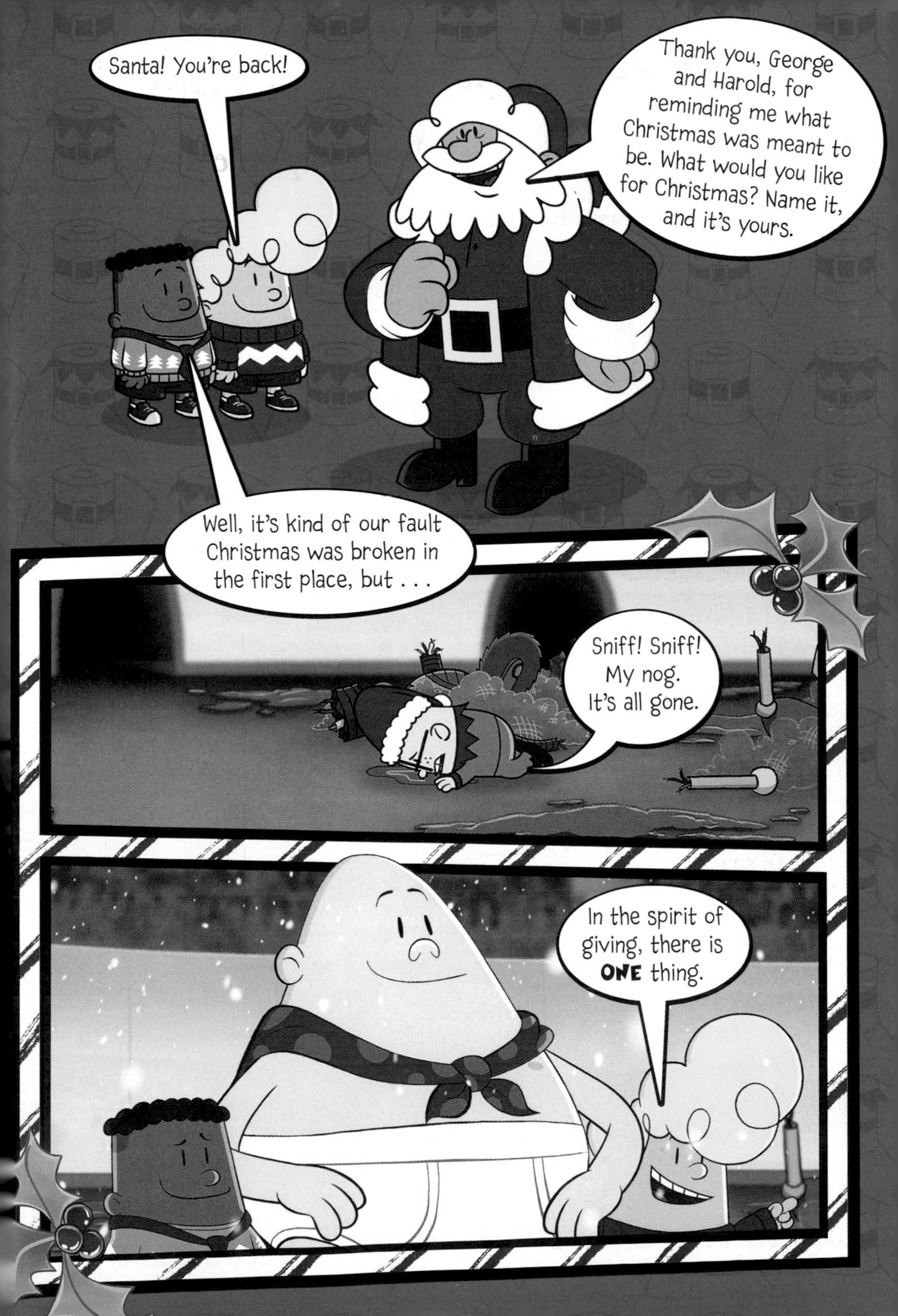
Santa! You're back!
Thank you, George and Harold, for reminding me what Christmas was meant to be. What would you like for Christmas? Name it, and it's yours.
Well, it's kind of our fault Christmas was broken in the first place, but . . .
Sniff! Sniff! My nog. It's all gone.
In the spirit of giving, there is ONE thing.

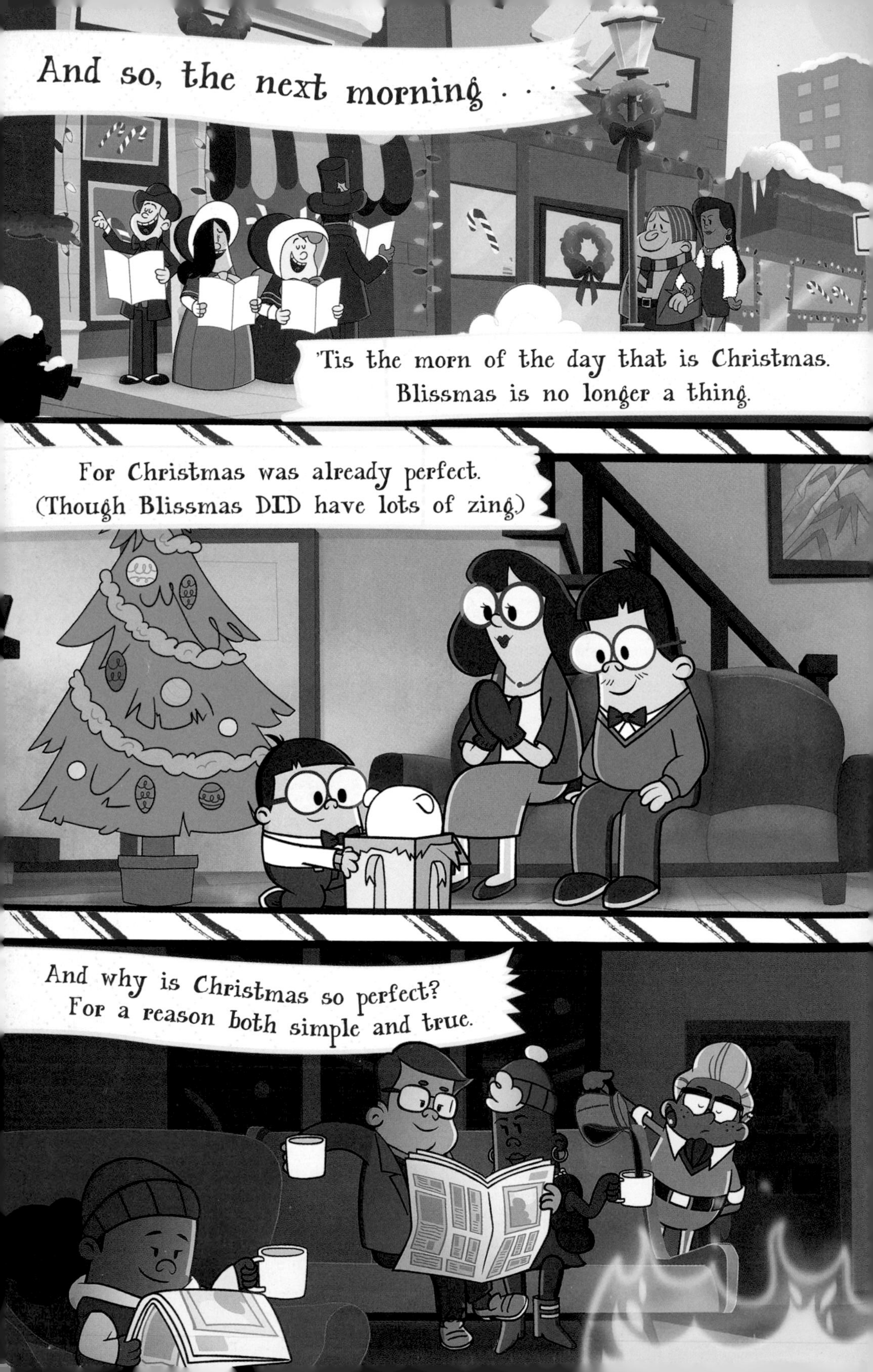
And so, the next morning . . .
'Tis the morn of the day that is Christmas.
Blissmas is no longer a thing.
For Christmas was already perfect.
(Though Blissmas DID have lots of zing.)
And why is Christmas so perfect?
For a reason both simple and true.

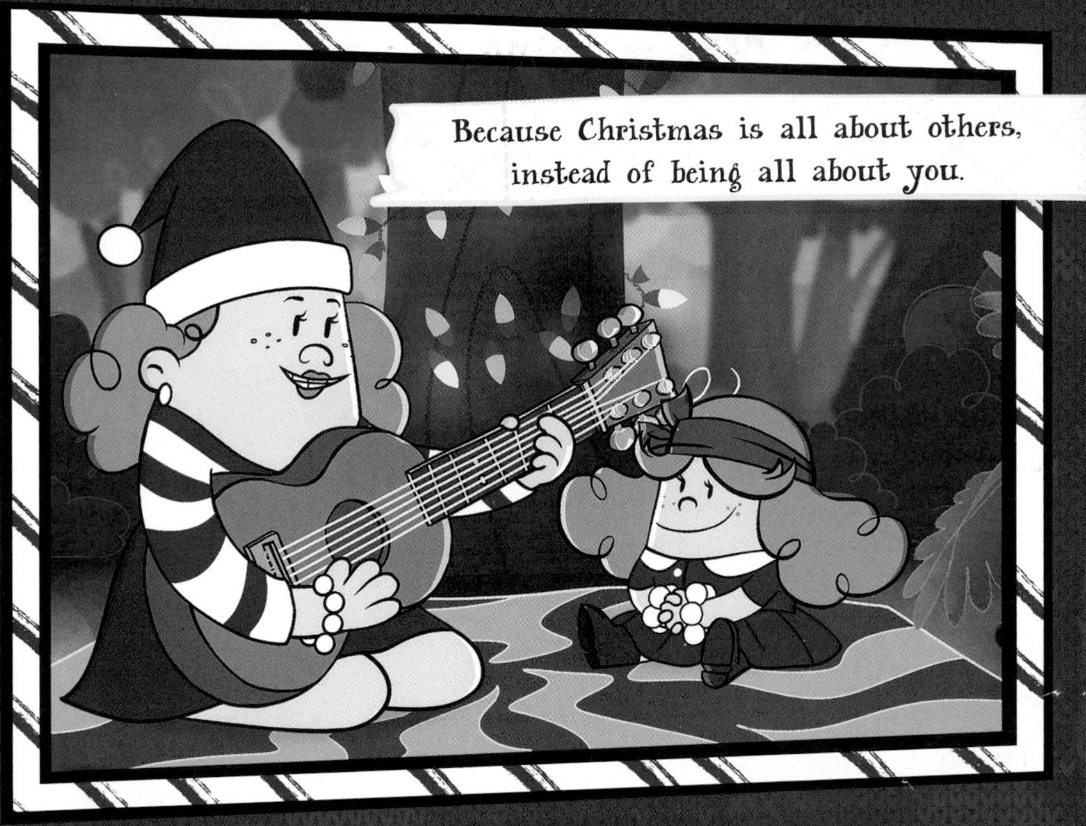
Because Christmas is all about others, instead of being all about you.

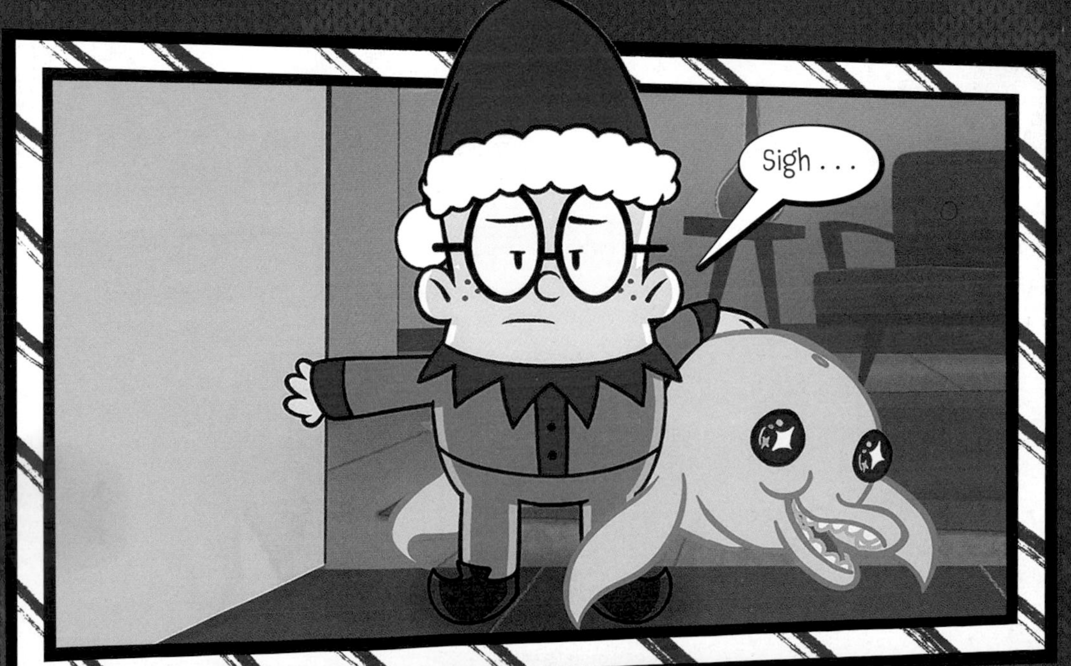
Sigh . . .

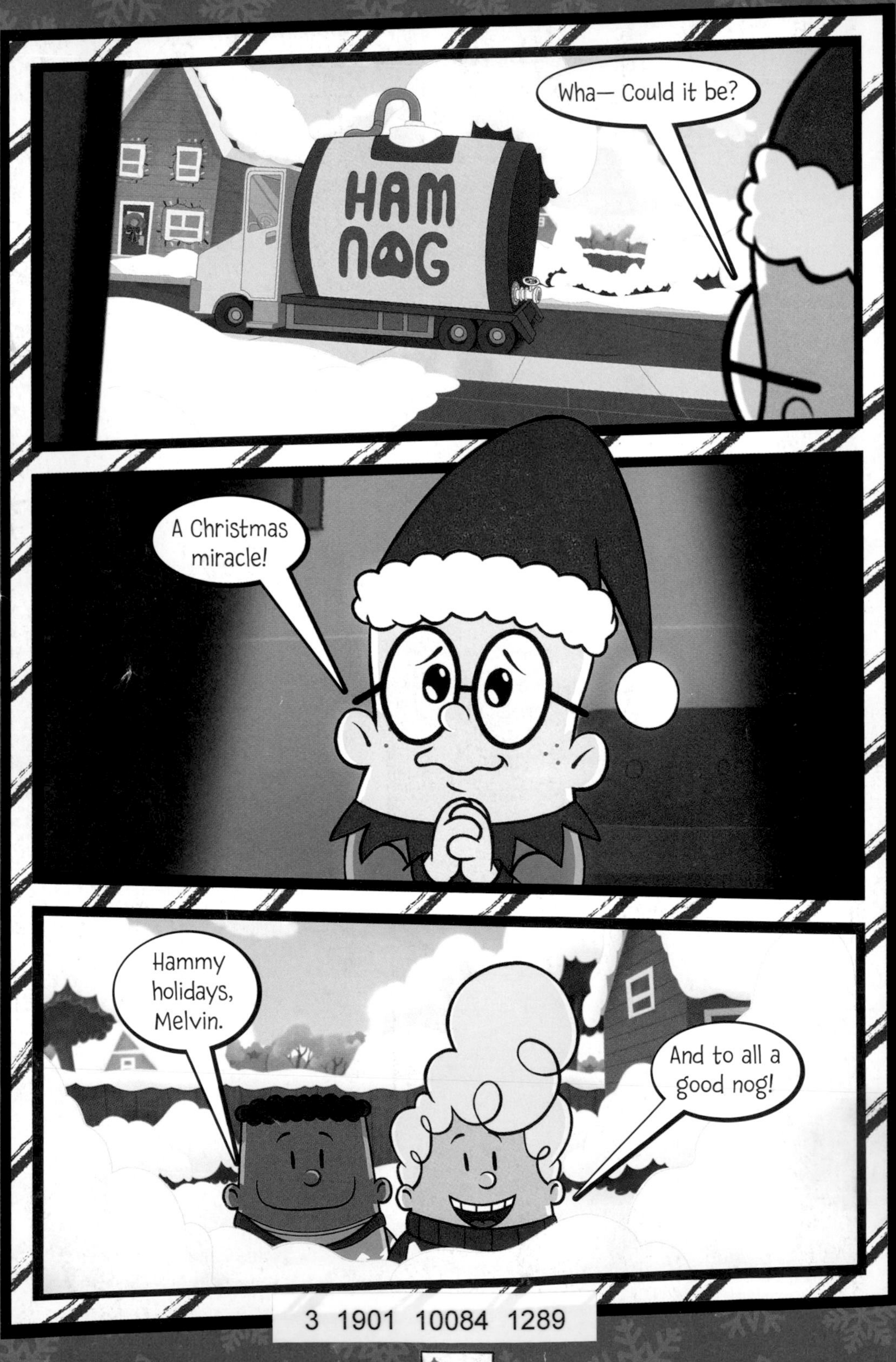
Wha— Could it be?
HAM NOG
A Christmas miracle!
Hammy holidays, Melvin.
And to all a good nog!